"The best of the melting pot. Inspira smallest state.

Michael Fine tells real stories of real people that make our community special. Telling Life experiences and life lessons that make an impact."

-Neil Steinberg, President & CEO, Rhode Island Foundation

"These stories are a grand landscape of the outer State and also the inner "state" of its residents—the secrets, dreams, wisdom, foolery, struggles and triumphs. The Good Doctor Fine is brilliant in his writing, large in his canvas, and deep in his understanding. If R.I. didn't have a Poet Laureate, now's the time to start. This is a triumph."

-Samuel Shem, M.D., Professor of Medicine and Humanities at NYU Medical School, author of *The House of God* and its sequel, *Man's 4th Best Hospital.*

"Michael Fine knows Rhode Island's people and places. He also knows what makes a good story. In this fine collection, he captures the hopes, dreams, fortunes and foibles of people across our quirky little state. You'll find someone you know here - maybe even yourself."

-Bill Harley, Singer, songwriter, storyteller, poet

"*Rhode Island Stories* captures the essence of Rhode Island's diversity and what makes our local communities so special, the people."

-Donald R Grebien, Mayor, Pawtucket RI

"Powerfully poignant, humane and embracing! Fine's latest work accomplishes what writers hope to do, but rarely accomplish...He opens the doors to many worlds, without interfering with any!"

-Marc Levitt is a Documentary Film Maker, Writer and Educator

"Dr. Fine peers into the ordinary lives of everyday people in his short stories that ask the question what if or why not. In my personal life and the multiple roles I play I often get lost in my own story fixated about the here and now without contemplating the bigger picture. When you read Dr. Fine's short stories they may also nudge you to think about your own life and what you can do to make this world a better place. This is a great read for those who are interested in stories placed in Rhode Island. For me the images of Rhode Island come alive in his stories and I believe they'll resonate for you too."

-Mario Bueno Executive Director Progresso Latino

"Dr. Michael Fine weaves together characters in stories in a way that reminds us that we have more in common than we have differences. Through his stories we are able to see ourselves as one people, indivisible after all."

-Nelly Gorbea, RI Secretary of State

" ...a beautiful depiction of Rhode Island... should gain interest from people all over America."

-Ray Rickman, Co-Founder and Executive Director, Stages of Freedom

"The best part of our city, and our state, is the incredible culture and diversity that's not only very present but openly celebrated. Stories of challenge and stories of overcoming. Stories of hard work, of hope, of family, and so much more. Through an unfiltered lens, *Rhode Island Stories* uniquely captures the depth of the narratives that often go untold, but quietly make up the very backbone of our communities."

-Maria Rivera, Mayor, City of Central Falls

Rhode Island Stories

Michael Fine

Rhode Island Stories
Copyright © 2019, 2020, 2021 Michael Fine
Produced and printed
by Stillwater River Publications.
All rights reserved. Written and produced in the
United States of America. This book may not be reproduced
or sold in any form without the expressed, written
permission of the author and publisher.
Visit our website at
www.StillwaterPress.com
for more information.
First Stillwater River Publications Edition
Library of Congress Control Number: 2021915195
Paperback ISBN: 978-1-955123-34-1
Hardcover ISBN: 978-1-955123-35-8
1 2 3 4 5 6 7 8 9 10
Written by Michael Fine
Published by Stillwater River Publications,
Pawtucket, RI, USA.

In memory of

Charles Chesnutt (1858-1932)
Lucius Garvin, MD (1841-1922)
and Bernard Lown, MD (1921-2021)

*"If you can see the invisible,
you can do the impossible"*

– Bernard Lown

Table of Contents

The First Violinist of Lowden Street 1

The Prisoner of Ideas 17

Amazing Grace 29

Job Lots 41

Isaiah on Route 6 49

Cancer 55

From All Men 63

21 Horses 73

Woke 85

God's Providence 101

Nero 121

Snow 133

The Death Spiral 153

The Deer Stand of the Dead Deer Hunter 165

The Social Determinants of Health 183

The Blind Emperor 193

Glossary 207

Introduction

Dr. Fine's writing, like all art, is the product of one person's processing and reporting on the human condition.

I wrote of Michael's book, *The Bull and Other Stories*, "Michael's writing is rhythmic with a jazz cadence, poignant, timely, and timeless, vivid detail -- but above all, Michael Fine is a storyteller — and a damn good one at that."

A "jazz cadence" anticipates the next note and is eager to get there, consciously tripping forward. "Poignancy" speaks to what is moving and at the same time slightly painful. "Timely" addresses immediate needs. "Timeless" looks to the future. And "vivid detail" implies a knowledge of the subject. All this is realized in his stories.

When I read Michael's fiction, I also think of his work in the community that is akin to his writing, projecting us forward, addressing the current needs of people, and at the same time working to create systems that anticipate and address the future needs of people. None of this can be accomplished without a story, a vivid story, one that is researched and clear. A story that is accessible and engaging.

We as a species are once again facing a paradigm shift. Like the industrial revolution, production and delivery of goods and of knowledge is changing. This paradigm shift must include considered change that is timely but also systemic.

None of this can be accomplished without stories. It is in the telling of stories that we engage the imaginations of the many. It is time for artists to help activate the activist to provide the images, sounds, and movements – the words of a revolution – a revolution that trips consciously forward into a new world that promises a more equitable society, one that allows for the possibility of the realization of the potential of all people. This is a dream that can no longer wait but must be realized for not just the survival of we as a people but also of that which sustains us, our planet.

Thank you, Michael for the stories that inspire a better and more conscious way of thinking, and more importantly, living.

Umberto Crenca
Artist, founder of AS220

Rhode Island Stories

The First Violinist of Lowden Street

To arrange the audition meant going places Sonia Bloch hadn't been able to go for a long time, places she never thought she'd go again. But Alexandra Jimenez was no ordinary student, and so it was worth opening old wounds and revisiting forgotten dreams.

Alexandra came to the Lowden Street house by herself one day in the early spring. She knocked. She was a slight girl carrying a violin case like so many others, about twelve, with olive skin, long dark hair and deep brown eyes that darted away between glances. Was this a place of lessons? she asked. It was a question no one had asked of Sonia before. Yes, of course, Sonia answered, inpatient, because Alexandra had disturbed her as she was paying bills, an activity Sonia hated. I would like to learn, Alexandra said. Who is this child? Sonia wondered, and she realized she must have appeared stern or even angry — but then no one had ever come to her door and asked for lessons in person. The mothers of prospective students usually called her to schedule a first lesson. Their children were almost always Jewish, Italian, Chinese, or Korean. The women who called were the wives of doctors and lawyers, women who were often doctors and lawyers themselves. They were second- and third-generation people, people who acted as if they had been in America forever, who spoke unaccented English and treated Sonia as if she were selling carpet or insurance, as if she had called *them* and not the other way around. As if she were not to be trusted. As if she were a servant or a tradeswoman. And not who she really was after all.

She brought the girl into her house and helped her off with her coat. Alexandra's instrument was a disaster, but then no child's violin is any good. The instrument had been in a closet. It looked as though no one had touched it in forty years. Sonia took out her second instrument and handed it to the girl. How did you find me? Sonia said, expecting to hear about a referral from the small city symphony orchestra where Sonia was a first violin or to hear about a school friend who was Sonia's student. I walk this way home, Alexandra said. I see other kids coming out of cars. With violins.

In fact, there *was* a school a few blocks away, and there was also a neighborhood of recent immigrants and boarded-up houses about a quarter-mile away in a different direction, down a hill and across a commercial street. A neighborhood of abandoned cars, broken pavement, and foreign grocery stores with garish flashing lights in their windows. Perhaps Alexandra found her way to Sonia's house completely on her own. Perhaps.

At least there were no bad habits to break. Alexandra had never held a violin. Sonia wondered if Alexandra had ever heard any of the music before. But she showed Alexandra, one small step at a time, as she talked about a process that, for Sonia, was as natural as breathing. Tighten and rosin the bow. The strange and uncomfortable placement of the left hand, so the fingers can move about the strings. How the instrument is placed against the neck, under the chin. Sonia remembered herself struggling to hold an instrument that was too large for her, in a cold room, in a four-story walk-up flat years ago. On the street below, the trams ran every few minutes. Where you looked out and saw the leafless trees, tram wires, trams and many people in the street, in the cold, weak light of the northern winter. I want you to do nothing but

hold the instrument for an hour
Sonia said, doubting that she wo
you one more time.

And then Sonia stood,
her. She stayed perfectly still l
of her moving at all, so Alex
Sonia drew the bow across a
this single note, a note shak
made every object in the room resona
teacup, bowl and lamp shade trembled slightly with the
music. I'll never see the girl again, Sonia thought, as Alexandra's wide
eyes turned from Sonia to the violin itself.

When Alexandra put her own instrument back in its case with
hands that were still too small to play, her movements were careful and
quick, as if she were handling an ancient family bible, an object of rev-
erence. She doesn't know you pay for lessons, Sonia realized, as she gave
the girl a time for the next week. Then Sonia stood at the storm door
and watched the girl walk down the walk to the street. It's only a few
minutes, Sonia told herself. These people are new in the country. They
have different music. Different traditions. Sweet child, but clueless. She
can't do much harm with that instrument, but it will frustrate her. She
won't be back.

It is strange to remember and strange to live again in the memories that come back without effort when you least expect them. Her
own beginning was completely different. Sonia had emerged in a world
of buildings, of trams and books and of the music everywhere. She remembered her parents taking turns reading stories to her at night, and
she remembered Mozart, Haydn, and Beethoven along with the stories.
Although now she could remember the melody and the phrasing of the

n she could recall the stories themselves. Peter

ates. Racing on the ice. Little boys falling through.

#4. Handel Concerto Grosso Opus 3 # 4 in F. The

. The radio and their record player which Sonia's father

e than anything else, the records smuggled in from Moscow

Aviv.

She was four. Her father didn't play well. The instrument came

om a pawnshop. He bought it early one spring when there was no food to spend money on. In the days before he lost his position at the university and began to work as a clerk in a dry cleaner's, before he left for America. The seam between the back and side was open and the fingerboard had come off. Sonia's mother was angry when he first brought it home. Wasteful, she said. Just fantasy. We need bread and meat. But Sonia's father, who could fix anything, found a friend with hide glue. He and his friend put the instrument back together and then there it was, restrung, ready to play and almost as big as Sonia herself.

One night, when Sonia's parents' friends had gathered and two of their friends were playing, Sonia lifted the violin. Four. She was only four years old and it was way past her bedtime. She stood up on a chair and said, I will play for you now a concert. Her parents and their friends laughed and applauded. Her father helped her hold the instrument for the first time. Sonia was so small that her left hand could barely reach the top of the violin's sound box so her father stood behind her and held the fingerboard. Even then the bow was too heavy for her small hand, so her father reached around and held her hand in his as he held the bow for her and placed her hand and the bow on the strings. But it was Sonia who drew the bow. Her father, in his wisdom, angled the bow just right. Sonia could still feel the heat from her father's warm chest as a note that was bigger than the whole house filled the room and spread through her body, sweet and clear and long.

The girl came back ten minutes past the appointed time. The narcissus was up against the white fence but had not finished blooming, and the sand on the streets that had been used to create traction when there was ice everywhere had not yet been swept away by rains and by street sweepers. Alexandra was wearing a red spring coat that was too long and too thin for the coolness of the day. Sonia helped her off with her coat and went to the kitchen to turn on the electric kettle so she could make Alexandra a cup of tea. When she came back to the parlor, Alexandra had the instrument out of the case and was holding the violin exactly as Sonia had shown her to hold it. She was standing in the window, so the slanted warm yellow light of later afternoon bathed her face and upper body.

When Sonia came into the room, Alexandra drew the bow over the G string. The note was long and clean. Then the girl up-bowed, a stirring and clear A. Sonia inhaled with the up-bowing and that breath, which was a breath of pure pleasure, suffused her body, so she stood taller and fuller than she had a few moments before. I did not tell you to play, Sonia said. I told you to just hold the instrument, nothing more. An hour a day. I did not give permission for the playing of notes. The little girl lowered the instrument, her face deflated, and Sonia hoped that the girl was not able to see any of the pleasure that Sonia felt in her face or the joy she felt inside herself. They do not know punctuality or how to follow directions, Sonia thought. She will not be back.

Alexandra came the next week at the appointed time. It was raining hard that day, and the thin red coat was soaked through. Alexandra's plain white blouse was grey on the shoulders, front and back now, glistening wet and cold to the touch. I'm getting you something to wear, Sonia said, and she brought a thick wool sweater from her bedroom. Change into this, Sonia said, the bathroom is down the hall, the second door on the left.

The girl is ludicrously thin, lost in that sweater, Sonia thought, as she put Alexandra's blouse in the dryer. But this time the girl stood and played all the open notes. Her blouse had dried by the time their time together was over.

It wasn't perfect. It never is. One day, Alexandra came early enough to see the previous student, a blond boy of twelve with a future as a scientist or a soccer player, finish his lesson. She saw the boy's mother get out her checkbook, scribble on it, tear off a check and hand the check to Sonia before they walked out. Sonia could sense Alexandra brooding about what she had seen. Alexandra was tense and distracted all during the lesson. Sonia waited for Alexandra to ask about what lessons cost, but the child didn't seem to have the words she needed. This girl needs to learn about how the world works, Sonia thought, although Sonia did not want either to cause the girl embarrassment or to let the girl off the hook.

In the summer, Alexandra missed a lesson, confirming what Sonia already knew. She's had it. She's done. No discipline. They don't know anything about this music. Why should she care? Her people listen to salsa and country music or top forty hits on the radio, and that is enough for them. She had wasted time giving away free lessons to a girl who could not possibly benefit from the attention. Just more wasted time in a life wasted on pursuits that went nowhere.

But the next week, Alexandra appeared at the appointed time. No words about the missed lesson passed between them. I am going to the Cape for two weeks, Sonia said, at the end of the lesson. Here is your assignment, week by week, so I will see you in not one, not two, but three Tuesdays from now, at the usual time. I expect you to be on time. If you must ever miss a lesson again, you must call me the day before. I require twenty-four-hour notice.

And then something occurred to Sonia. She went into the kitchen where she kept her business cards and brought back a card and a pencil. This is my name, Sonia said. And this is my telephone number, she said, as she circled her number on the card. They had been working together for four months, and Sonia realized that Alexandra didn't know the first thing about her, not even her name, and Sonia didn't know the first thing about Alexandra. Then Sonia went back to the kitchen and found an index card. Print your name, address and telephone number here, Sonia said. That way if I ever must cancel, I can call you the day before as well.

That card, written in pencil, in block letters that were not precisely formed, would live ever-after on the corkboard next to the telephone in Sonia's hall. Next to the cards of the plumber, the electrician, the taxicab company, the police and fire departments and the number of rescue, on the corkboard where Sonia's eyes rested whenever she answered the telephone. The must-have information Sonia needed to maintain her life.

In two years, Alexandra became brilliant, the student all teachers wish for, the student who would surpass her. Alexandra was not a great violinist by any means. Not yet. But she was a great student. She learned quickly and in her fingers there somehow appeared emotion, the one aspect of musicianship that Sonia did not know how to teach. This girl, who barely spoke and whose command of English wasn't certain, understood in some part of her what the music meant, and that understanding came out through her fingers and in her phrasing. Her technique was good, yes, and she rapidly developed the strength and dexterity to play, strength and dexterity that comes only from practicing three, four, even six hours a day. But this girl had something more. She had the music hidden in her soul, and it sprang from her as if it were caged and struggling to be released from that thin, simple, lost body.

Sonia was a good teacher, but soon Alexandra would need a great teacher. Someone who could frighten her and drive her, but also a teacher quietly connected to great performers and great orchestras. A teacher quietly sought out by the world's great ones, who come from near and far to take a private lesson, looking for a new tone or to polish a texture, so they can go from confident and musical to great and stirring; from polite applause to twenty minutes of a standing ovation. Alexandra would have to go to Boston or New York to live, and she would have to give her whole life to the music, to do what Sonia had been unable to do, and to realize what Sonia had been unable to realize.

Sonia's first teacher had made those connections for Sonia when she herself was twelve, just a girl living in Buda. She had been thin herself, thin and quite pale, just old enough to understand the paleness of her parents and know the meaning of the numbers on their arms, and just aware enough to know their anxieties and sleeplessness, which became her anxieties and her sleeplessness. Sonia was old enough to remember the red stars, the red flags, and the huge public statues, and also old enough to remember when the trams ran every five minutes and were free. Old enough to remember always knowing that there were many places and many schools where she could not go because of who she was, but too young to remember the Russian tanks when they rolled through the streets in 1956. There was always music in their flat, even when there was little joy.

Sonia's first teacher brought her to Simhousen when she was twelve. The great man looked through her as she took her instrument out of the case. Is this one strong enough? she sensed he asked himself as she lifted her instrument. He was thinking, will she stand up to what I am going demand that she does, or will she crack? What I will demand on top of everything else. In spite of it. In those years no one spoke of what they had lived through because all of them had lived through it together, and words about it conveyed nothing, compared to what it meant to have survived.

But Simhousen was shocked when Sonia played. She was so thin. Simhousen was accustomed to precision from the students brought to him to audition. He knew virtuosity. But Sonia surprised him. The story of what they had experienced came through her even though she had not experienced any of it herself. The pain. The fear. The loneliness. The cold and the starvation and the exhaustion. The loss. The endless losses. Their survival, yes the survival but only as a fragment of what had been before. A whole world entirely lost. It was all there in her playing. Miraculous. Simhousen stood up while she played and then he paced. Five years of work, endless work, he said. And then perhaps. Only perhaps. I am not certain she will last.

Now, the great teacher, the great man, was a woman, Vivienne Liung. She was ten years younger than Sonia and was better known as a teacher than she was as a performer. She had studied with the great teachers who taught Sonia's generation, she had performed all over the world, she had won the major competitions and then she had withdrawn from performing to teach. She had also studied with Simhousen, though in the last years of the great man's life.

Vivienne was coming to Providence in November for thirty-six hours as a guest soloist with the orchestra. The orchestra would rehearse on its own for six weeks before the performance and then would rehearse once with Vivienne the night before the concert. Vivienne would give a masterclass in the early afternoon on the day of the concert. Then a radio interview. Then a stop at Brown to be on a panel. Then a performance at the Vets, and then off to New York by train in the morning.

Sonia, who had been first violin in the Rhode Island Philharmonic for 30 years, heard in May that Vivienne was coming. The pieces were announced, the scores distributed, and the orchestra would begin rehearsals for those pieces in early October. It was a Sonia's hobby, playing in that orchestra. A little orchestra in a little provincial town. Just to keep her hand in, and to attract students. Teaching kept Sonia alive now.

There was an intermediary in London, a friend who Sonia had played with in Budapest before she emigrated. Emails went back and forth. I have a promising student Vivienne should hear. The friend in London had to remind Vivienne who Sonia was, who she studied with, who she had been and who she could have become.

Vivienne finally responded. There are a few minutes in the late afternoon. Have her come to my hotel. Have her prepare three difficult pieces. She should expect me to grill her. To push her. To try to break her. There is some of the old man in me, Vivienne wrote, once she understood Sonia's lineage.

By this time the girl had become more presentable, but there was still a part of Alexandra that Sonia didn't know. Many parts. Alexandra had achieved technical mastery of all the pieces Sonia rehearsed with her. She stood correctly. She breathed correctly. Her tone was perfect and her phrasing was immaculate, so good that Sonia didn't understand how she had come by it. As her technique improved, Alexandra had learned to look the part of a performer. Sonia brought her to hear the orchestra when they played, to rehearsals and to performances, picking her up in front of her house in that neighborhood that was both close by and so far away, and dropping her there after the performance, before Sonia joined the others for coffee or vodka and to decompress. Alexandra took a black skirt Sonia gave her, added a white blouse, and learned to look perfectly respectable. Her long dark brown hair was now brushed back and hung almost to her waist, reflecting the order and luster of hundreds of brush strokes. Her ochre skin added depth to the whiteness of her blouse. Her almost black eyes, opaque and subterranean at the same time, made her appear close and mysterious at once.

But Sonia didn't know how Alexandra lived. Sonia had never been in Alexandra's house, which was on a street that few people knew. It was a pale green and grey-white triple-decker with almost no yard, a broken up cement driveway, and a grape arbor made from old iron pipes in front. The tiny porch with three rotting steps and no handrail led to two doors. Next to each door was a line of doorbells and nameplates, but most of the name cards were scratched out, written over or just blank. Alexandra was almost always on the porch, outside, waiting when Sonia came for her. When Sonia let Alexandra off at home after a concert, she stayed in front of the house, the car running and the lights on until Alexandra had the key in the lock and the door opened because there was no working porch-light, and because, well, just to be safe.

Sonia didn't know Alexandra's people. No mother had ever brought Alexandra for a lesson or picked her up after the lesson was over. Alexandra answered the door herself whenever Sonia rang it. No one else – no sister, father, uncle, or a grandmother ever came to the door to say Alexandra will be down in a moment, why don't you come in.

The concert started at eight. Come to my hotel at 5:45 and I'll listen to your student, Vivienne had written. The hotel is next to the Vets. I'll listen, and then we can walk to the concert hall together.

I'll come and get you at five, Sonia told Alexandra. Be ready, Sonia said. Don't be late. Dress appropriately. Everything depends on this day.

As she drove to Alexandra's house on the day of the audition, Sonia remembered how she thought her life would be after Simhousen, after the great man blessed her, and how different her life was from those dreams. She thought, I will practice all the time. I will perform in Budapest but also in Prague, Vienna, Berlin, Frankfurt, Moscow, Venice and Tel Aviv. And then in London, Boston and New York. I will have a large airy flat overlooking the Danube with its own practice room, and I will marry a conductor or a great cellist. We will have a country house. Before long I will teach master classes of my own and learn to frighten the best students, so we find and train the great ones, frightening off those without an inner being made of steel, and leaving the others to give lessons or play in the orchestras of small cities or to do something else entirely, to become computer programmers or dermatologists or engineers.

Sonia practiced all the time. She won the competitions that must be won. She performed with the orchestras and got the kind of reviews soloists dream of. One step led to another, which was certain to lead to a third. First a chair in the orchestra. Then a solo career.

But when Sonia was ready to step up, all the chairs in the orchestra were full. None of the violinists were retiring. The generation who Sonia should have replaced had been killed off or had fled twenty years before. Those who filled their seats, whose playing was perhaps not at the level of the pre-war years, were in those seats nonetheless and didn't plan on leaving for another twenty years. Prague or Moscow, perhaps. But nothing at all in Budapest.

Then there was political turmoil and with turmoil came years of shortages before the wall came down, and then came a few years of chaos and more shortages.

In those years of turmoil, the established pathways to a secure place had fallen apart. You couldn't simply go from Budapest to Moscow anymore and in Moscow earn the respect needed to travel internationally. Instead, you had to emigrate and start all over in London, New York or Tel Aviv.

Then suddenly it became possible to travel and even to emigrate.

Sonia met a chemist after one of her performances, a chemist who knew the music. When Leonid courted her, he promised London and New York. But after they married, and there was Sasha and Karl, they came to Rhode Island, not New York, for a university position. With the university position came the undergraduates and the graduate students, too many of whom were young women, and then, in a flash, Sonia's imagined life was gone.

Sonia parked outside Alexandra's house. There were no lights on inside the house, but it there was still daylight. Alexandra was not waiting on the porch. Sonia honked her horn. It was five of five. There was still time.

Vivienne and Sonia walked together from the hotel to the concert hall.

We know that only a very few will progress. The process of finding and training those few is long and difficult. The life itself has many limitations. Many doors have to remain closed along the way. The discipline is withering. Some doors should never even be imagined, let alone tried. There is no shame in trying, in testing.

Vivienne and Sonia did not speak of these things, of course. They spoke only of Simhousen. They both remembered the strength of the great man's grip when he shook a person's hand and the power of his embrace when he hugged you after not seeing you for a long time. How when he held you, how he seemed to be holding onto life itself.

Sonia, before and after her apology, could not think and she could not feel. Her ability to feel anything ended forever while she was standing on that porch, as she rang the bell and knocked on that door again and again at five-fifteen, until five-thirty. A short unshaven man in a tee-shirt, wearing only green plaid undershorts, stumbled to the other door, barely awake or barely sober or both, having been woken by Sonia's voice and her persistent hard rapping. No here, he said, when he saw her knocking on the other door. No home. And then he turned away, closed his door, and walked back up the stairs.

Even so, Vivienne treated Sonia with respect. Sonia had studied with the old man. Vivienne knew now who Sonia once was. And who she could have been.

The concertmaster came on stage as the orchestra was warming up, each instrument making a note or two to test the precision of their tuning. Together they created a bright cacophony of hopes and expectations. The concertmaster stood, raised his bow, and the instruments quieted. He sat. The conductor came on the stage to applause, waved and then bowed. The conductor went to the microphone and said a few words about the program and each piece. Then he introduced Vivienne, who took the stage confidently, wearing a low-cut black silk dress and pearls. She stood in a spotlight, waiting her cue.

Sonia sat stage left, in the row of first violins.

The conductor raised his baton.

Sonia drew her bow across the strings. The note Sonia played was sweet, long and clear. It came not from her instument but from inside Sonia herself, from her chest and pelvis, from her belly and her back, from her thighs and shoulders. Her body and soul wrapped itself around that note, perfecting its pitch and intonation as the note went free, tuned by every part of her. Sonia hated Alexandra in that moment and loved her. She hated life and loved life, both at the same time.

The note joined itself to the timbre and tone of the orchestra's rising sound, which felt as if it was ascending to heaven itself.

And then the note disappeared.

The Prisoner of Ideas

No man or woman can be trusted, thought Sonia Cano, but this one certainly is something of a distraction. I fall into the same rabbit-hole every time. They pique my interest one day. The next thing I know it's two years later and I hear their voice coming out of my mouth, their thoughts are in my brain, and suddenly I realize that what I'm saying and thinking has nothing to do with what I actually think or what I actually feel and then I bolt.

There was nothing special about the house on Congress Street and Sonia didn't give a damn about gentrification. It was a triple-decker, like every other house in Central Falls. Sonia bought it because it was cheap and because the numbers worked. You get two tenants, they pay the rent, the rent covers the mortgage, and you live for free. Or better than free, to be honest, because you can charge all sorts of expenses to the house and make that income invisible to the tax man, even though it comes in as cash every month. Why would a woman not buy a house?

But to Babatunde, Sonia's house represented everything that was right and wrong with America, everything that was right and wrong with democracy, and everything that was right and wrong with Sonia herself, although before Babatunde came into her life, Sonia had never seriously considered that there was anything wrong with her at all.

Sonia thought she was done with relationships, just done, once and for all, and so she went back to college to finish her degree. She had three excellent children, each more interesting than the next, who were finally now old enough so they didn't need their mother's attention every second. She had her sisters and brothers, whose difficulties provided plenty of distraction in her life. The office ran like clockwork — there were plenty of people answering the phones — and Sonia had a list of per-diems — mostly college kids and Uber drivers — she'd ring up at the last moment if one of her regulars called in sick. The last two men had given her children and were steady enough to do their share when she needed someone to drive a child to school or pick up from soccer, but they had both fallen off the wagon one way or the other, one to another woman, one to beer and other women, but she had learned something from being with each of them and had no regrets. Her relationship with Sofia had become so complicated that it was too much to think any more about it. So now it is my time, Sonia thought. I'll finish college one course at a time. Then I'll go to law school at night. The lawyers in my office don't have any better sense than I do. They just got to this country first and they make a whole lot more money than I do for doing a whole lot less work.

But then there was Babatunde, who Sonia hadn't counted on meeting, poor beautiful Babatunde, the adjunct professor and poet, the man who would be a student for the rest of his life, who was pretty, brilliant, full of soul and would never earn a living. What did she see in him?

They are building a new train station in Pawtucket, Babatunde said. Gentrification! The rich will be coming from Boston by train! They will buy up all the property! Property values will go through the roof! Taxes will go up! You and your kids, you won't be able to live in Central Falls anymore! Central Falls will be for millennials! They will destroy our communities! Where will our people go? How will our people live?

There was something about Babatunde's blue-brown dark skin and beautiful brown eyes that Sonia could not stop thinking about. It made no sense. But oh, how that man had soul.

The first time they met for coffee it was to discuss her paper on Chaucer. Babatunde was earnest and polite. He focused on her usage and her construction, not on her ideas. Outline, he said. Think out what you want to say first, then say it. Short direct sentences with active verbs and no adverbs. Don't copy someone else's style. You don't need to sound important. Just say what you think and be yourself. I don't write well in English, Sonia said. I think in English but with Spanish style. Flowery. A little overblown, like a woman who wears too much make-up. You are hiding, buried under words and sentences, Babatunde said. English thinking is cool, not hot, Sonia said. And Babatunde raised his eyes to meet hers for the first time. Chaucer is quite hot, Babatunde said. But I understand what you mean. Yoruba thinking is also different. Complex. Textured, elegant, full of hidden meanings, and English thinking has none of that richness. I'm sorry this course is so Eurocentric. You might prefer the Latin and Central Americans: García Márquez, Clarice Lispector, Octavio Paz, Isabel Allende, Roberto Bolaño. Laura Esquivel, Neruda, and even Vargas Llosa, that capitalist. And Garcia Lorca. Yes García Lorca. Read them in Spanish, I think. Except Lispector who you will have to read in translation and is very difficult but worth the effort. But read the women first. I don't have time to read, Sonia said, because of children, my house and work. I pray I can get through the reading and papers for this course. But my writing and thinking, I have no time for this, it takes so much time... That is why I, as a teacher, have office hours, Babatunde said. To teach. To make it simpler for you to write. Can I send you my papers in draft form? Sonia said. Better yet, send outlines first, Babatunde said. And we will meet once a week.

Once a week soon became more than that.

But then an unexpected difficulty came between them. Babatunde came to the house to have dinner one night with Sonia and her kids. Sonia went all out — aripas, chicken, beef, chicharron, morcilla, costilla, tostones, fried yucca with cheese – not that she was cooking to impress, of course. She only wanted to show Babatunde that she was good at something, that her clumsy sentence construction and poor word choice didn't represent the full range of her knowledge and abilities.

Babatunde didn't eat much but Sonia's kids loved him anyway. He had a poet's appreciation for childhood, and he became a child again as soon as they sat down to dinner — he popped his cheek, in and out — when Sonia poured out wine. He made fun of Sonia by speaking first in Pig Latin and then in Middle English. He went from saying easplay asspay ethay altsay to Whan that Aprille with his shoures soote The Droghte of Marche hath perced to the roote, which he made Sonia translate for them, and then say the next four lines of the prologue, and then made Yolanda say the next two lines and Hector say the next two lines and he even got Jasmine, who was only eight, to say a line. Before long Sonia's kids were listening to the whole prologue to the Canterbury Tales. They loved every word and every note of what sounded like music, and Sonia could feel those kids falling in love with Babatunde's soul the way she had. They had fathers who were good men, but Babatunde was just on a different plane of being. Sonia suddenly felt somehow thrilled to be alive.

Later, when they were together, when Sonia teased him about not eating much, it came out that Babatunde was a vegetarian, and couldn't eat much of what she made and served. He had an elegant way of telling her that. He didn't say anything about what he would or wouldn't eat. He just talked about how much he liked the arepa and the yucca, about how much he liked reciting Chaucer to her children, and how much he liked watching them eat the rice and beans. She understood. Next time there will be more vegetables, she said. I make mean maduros, she said, and a fantastic lentil soup.

So Sonia couldn't believe it when Babatunde told her he wouldn't come back to her house ever again.

"My children loved you," she said. It was a Friday, and they were in his office at RIC, in the tiny little cubicle they gave adjuncts which was jammed with books and papers. A desk. A desk-lamp. Shelves and two chairs, one on each side of a desk.

"I loved your children. They have life and energy, and a mother with heart and imagination," Babatunde said. "But your house is in the danger zone for gentrification, and I can't go back there. When I was with you, I could hear the cries of the people who will be dispossessed, the people who have come to Central Falls from all over the globe, from Honduras and El Salvador and the Dominican Republic, from Cape Verde and Liberia and Nigeria and Mali after tremendous suffering and who are about to be forced to flee again, just after they reconstituted their lives. It is too much pain to bear."

"The train station isn't built yet," Sonia said. "They haven't even broken ground."

"This is not the point," Babatunde said. "The capitalists and the materialists are rising out of the bowels of the earth, coming up from of the lower depths, swarming and getting ready to pounce. First they buy up the old brick mill buildings on Clay, Pine and Barton Streets. Then they buy up the triple-deckers and make them over into housing for Brown and RISD students. Our people, who already take two buses to get to work, will have to take three buses. They will have to move to Johnston, West Warwick, and Danielson where they are not wanted, where there are no others like them, where no one else wants to live. We must rise up! The time to stop the process is now! The souls of displaced children are already calling out!"

"Please tell me exactly how you're not coming to my house is rising up?" Sonia said. "Do you expect me to sell my house and displace my children today? For something that may or may not happen in five years? You are saying something else. You are saying my children and I are not good enough for you. I may not write English well, but I understand what you are saying loud and clear."

Then Babatunde got on his knees in front of her, his hands locked together, and bowed his head in prayer. The door to the cubicle was open. Someone might see!

"I am saying that we will take this on together. I pray for your forgiveness. To me, ideas have souls. Some are the congealed pain of our history, the history of the oppressed, and some days I feel that pain in the center of my being. But you are my liberation. In you I see the beauty of all our people, the story of people who were cast down but find in themselves the strength to rise up, the seeds that germinate in cool darkness and push their way up through dirt and decay into the light."

What can a woman say to a man like that? Babatunde's words made her skin tingle. Sonia leaned over and kissed him on the forehead. She took his clasped hands in hers, lifted him from his knees, and stood up herself. Then she closed the door.

After that every Friday night, when she didn't have to work in the morning, her sister Claudette, who had two little kids of her own, came to stay with Sonia's kids so Sonia could be with Babatunde at his place in North Providence. He lived over a butcher shop, next to a lemonade stand, in a place that was in the middle of nowhere, a place that would never be gentrified because no one in their right mind would ever want to live there. Still, that place was fine for one night a week, and Babatunde somehow made Sonia's soul glad and let her body be at peace.

She took the summer off. There wasn't any rush. The plan had always been to take one course at a time. Her kids needed her attention in the summer. It was going to take her six or seven years to finish her degree anyway. Some days work just didn't matter that much. It was better to load the kids in the car in the late afternoon and drive to the beach, to Horseneck or East Matunuck, when you could slip though after the traffic had come and gone and park for free. It was the same beach after six that it was in the morning when traffic filled Route 4 and the fifteen dollar-a-car parking lots jammed with cars, the same lime green sea grass moving in waves with the wind, the same tawny white sand, still warm on your feet from the day's sun but not too hot to walk on, and the same glorious ocean, which was still ready to snatch you away from yourself, lift you, twirl you around mercilessly and throw you wherever without restraint.

She registered for the fall semester in August. Disappointing as it was, she just didn't need another English course for pre-law. Best to find a course that met twice a week and late in the afternoon, but one that wasn't too dry and where she might learn something she actually needed to know. POL 201.The Development of American Democracy. POL 202 American Government. PHIL 205. Introduction to Logic. ECON 200 Introduction to Economics. HIST 201 US History to 1877. Too many choices! Babatunde said he'd help with her writing whatever she chose, and he forgave her for her choice: ECON 200. But he brought her a new book to read every time they were together. And talked about the papers he was grading for ENGL 207 American Literature Beginnings to the Present. He hated teaching Dreiser and Steinbeck, but loved Whitman, Emily Dickinson, Richard Wright, William Carlos Williams, Amiri Bakara, Allen Ginsberg and Martin Espada. Hope, Babatunde said. America is hope, however irrational, and the inappropriate expectation of justice in a world where no justice has ever existed.

Sonia found herself waking at 3 AM and reading the books Babatunde brought. I don't have time for this, Sonia thought. I need to be alert, on my game all day long. But something about the summer's heat was disquieting, that woke her and forced her awake, something she couldn't quite put her finger on, something that kept eating at her. Even so Sonia's brain stayed in gear all day long, even when, in a late afternoon meeting, she felt her eyelids get heavy. I can do this, Sonia told herself. I must resist. And she'd stand and command more attention by standing, even as she brought herself back from the brink.

One Monday at the end of summer, when the nights were still hot and the drone of air-conditioners drowned out the rumble and groan of the trucks on Route 95, Sonia awoke in the middle of the night and dressed. There was no light in the sky. She checked on the children who were still sleeping. Seventeen minutes there, she thought. Seventeen minutes back. I can be back in my house and back in my bed before six-thirty. But I must know.

She drove to North Providence.

There is an unusual peace in the city before dawn in the summer. Nothing moves. Everyone is sleeping. Everything is blue, grey and brown, as if standing in the fog. No one looks, no one sees, and no one knows. There is enough light to see what you need to see. You can learn what you need to learn before anyone knows you have been there and gone.

Babatunde's beat up old blue Saturn was parked at the curb, sandwiched between other old cars: Fords and old Toyotas, Kias and step vans, the tired cars of the poor, cars that spend every night on the street. The light in his kitchen was on. What have I learned? Sonia wondered. Only that his car is here and his kitchen light is on. Nothing else. She parked in front of a fire hydrant across the street and sat for a few minutes. Then she drove home.

It was raining the next night when Sonia awoke, a wind-driven rain without thunder or lightening that spattered and clicked on the glass windowpanes. The children were sleeping. She dressed and hurried out. She eased the front door closed so the door nestled and did not slam and so the lock closed instead of clicked. She guided the screen door back into its frame so it didn't bang. Then she drove to North Providence in the rain. She couldn't see much, of course. The wind-blown rain brought darkness, made her headlights murky, and made the tree branches hanging over the road into angry spirits that wanted to smother Sonia, her car and the road itself.

Sonia didn't see Babatunde's car at first. Dread, sadness, despair and anger, the emotions that had been waking her, grabbed her throat, eyes, kidneys and the pit of her stomach. But then, as she drove past the house to find a place to turn, she saw the blue Saturn parked half a block away from the butcher shop. When she turned and parked in front of the fire hydrant again, she saw that the light was on again in Babatunde's kitchen, partially obscured by the branches and leaves of a big maple that were swaying with the wind and rain.

Sonia awoke Wednesday night but she stayed home. She paced inside her bedroom for an hour until her feet got cold, so she made herself a cup of coffee. She sat in front of a window at her kitchen table and stared at the pink vinyl siding of the house next door. This is craziness, she told herself. What am I doing? I don't own the man. I'm not sure I even really want him. He wants his space. I want my space. There is nothing to be learned from going over there in the middle of the night. I can't change him. I can barely control myself.

But she woke again Thursday night with the same panic, dread, sadness, despair, and anger she had been waking with for weeks. She drove to North Providence. The kitchen light was on. But there was no car. She drove slowly down the street two and three times. Then she circled the block once, and then circled it again. There were no open parking spaces in front of Babatunde's house but there were plenty of open parking spaces on the street that ran parallel to Babatunde's street.

She drove further up the street and circled the blocks on both sides of the street and the block behind Babatunde's block. She parked again in the space in front of the fire hydrant.

Then she collapsed. You couldn't tell by looking at Sonia that anything was different. But inside her, everything was different, as if her soul was made of sugar or salt that was pouring away through a funnel, spilling onto the ground until there was nothing left inside. Her breath got short. She sobbed once as she put her head in her hands, but she held onto the world nonetheless. I am stronger than this, she thought. I will not cry. And then she drove home.

The old blue Saturn was parked in front of the house on Congress Street. Babatunde was asleep inside it, a book on his chest.

He jumped when Sonia rapped on the car window. He appeared confused, his eyes unfocused, as if he didn't know where he was, how he had gotten there, or even who Sonia was. He found his glasses, which were sitting on the top of his head, and put them on. Sonia didn't wait for him to roll down the window. She marched around the car and tugged on the handle of the passenger side door, which was locked, two or three times, until Babatunde understood enough about where he was, who she was, and where they were to unlock the door, which she opened and then she came inside the car.

"What are you doing here?" Sonia said. "It is five o'clock in the morning."

"I fell asleep," Babatunde said.

"That is apparent," Sonia said. "You are sleeping in a car in front of my house, on my street, in my city. It is five o'clock in the morning. You did not answer my question. What, just what, are you doing here?"

"Why are you angry?" Babatunde said.

"I just left your house. Your car was not parked in front of your house. You have other interests, it appears," Sonia said.

"I am parked in front of *your* house," Babatunde said. "On *your* street. In *your* city. Not anywhere else. I saw you across the street from my house, in my city, every night, parked in front of the fire hydrant, when I got up to write. And then you didn't come last night. So I came here to see for myself, to surprise you and perhaps to talk. But then I fell asleep."

"You refused to come to my house," Sonia said. "You have ideas about gentrification and the dispossessed."

"Those were just ideas," Babatunde said. "And not particularly good ones after all. So I came here tonight to surprise you."

Sonia paused and suddenly she could see and feel something she hadn't seen or felt before. These were not particularly beautiful words or particularly beautiful ideas but once again her skin was tingling.

"Would you like to come in for coffee?" she said. "It's almost time for breakfast."

What thrills Sonia most today is not who lives where. What thrills Sonia most today is knowing that she has someone close who listens. Sometimes she writes papers for class and Babatunde edits those papers. He doesn't give her ideas. He helps her say what she believes instead of hiding it behind words.

And sometimes Sonia slips into one of Babatunde's classes toward the end of the class period. She doesn't come to protect her investment by walking out with him arm in arm. She comes only to hear what he has to say, and to listen to the beauty of his ideas, which are just a little less beautiful than his rich and imaginative soul.

Babatunde comes with Sonia on Saturdays in the spring. She coaches soccer. He sits in the stands and reads, or sometimes talks to the parents of other players about immigration, gentrification, justice and democracy. But most other times he keeps his ideas to himself and is pleased how much he is learning about unconditional love.

The world now seems full of life and hope, despite its many difficulties.

Amazing Grace

The crisis of the moment was rent. And that Sheila wouldn't open her door.

Grace stood on the front step of Shelia's trailer off Newport Avenue, near where Building 19 ½ used to be, and banged on Shelia's door. She had called first. The flimsy aluminum front wall of the trailer shook each time the heel of Grace's hand hit the door. No doorbell. Just wires next to the door drooping toward the little rectangular spot where the doorbell itself used to be.

It was October. The days had already shortened. A light rain was falling. Wet leaves were everywhere. They coated the ground, the step, and the pink and blue awnings over the front windows of other trailers. There were wet leaves on the hoods and roofs of the cars, on the tiny lawns, on the lawn furniture and the grills and barbeques that sat beside those tiny lawns. The leaves were yellow, red, and green. The air smelled sweet, like maple sugar.

Shelia, a woman of seventy-two with lung cancer, hadn't paid her rent in six months. She spent her rent money on cigarettes and booze. She was going be evicted in six days unless somebody did something. There was a social worker at the Department of Human Services who had money to keep people from being thrown out in the street, but in order to get that money, Shelia needed to get herself to the Human Services office on Roosevelt Avenue and fill out a form. The office was two miles away. Two-page form. Shelia needed to bring her rent checks and her electric and phone bills. All Grace needed to do was to get Shelia out of bed, out of the house, over to Roosevelt Avenue and get her to fill out one two-page form. No need to get evicted. At least not today. Not rocket science.

Shelia was a disaster, like most of Grace's clients — what happens to people when you let bad genes, bad choices, lousy bureaucracy and a world that just doesn't give a damn run things for a couple of generations, not that Grace's own life and choices were so great. Shelia was behind in her rent. They were threatening to turn off her electric. There was the lung cancer, a thousand doctors' appointments and chemo to be scheduled, getting Shelia back and forth — and all that medicine Shelia couldn't afford. There was the man, that low life Shelia let live with her — twenty years younger than she was, addicted to Percocets, who didn't work, who stole Shelia's drugs and sold them on the street and who just hung around hoping Shelia would die, hoping he'd get the trailer and the car. The damn trailer wasn't even Shelia's. It was a rental.

The trailer was a mess — papers piled on every table and chair, open cans left standing on the counters, black plastic garbage bags half full of clothes, or garbage, or cans of food that had never been put away, strewn over the floor. The car was a beat-up Dodge Avenger from the eighties with a broken off antenna and a radio that didn't work.

Shelia had a family, sort of, a collection of old wounds and massive disappointments. She had two daughters. One lived in Cranston, had three kids and worked as a waitress. Daughter number two was divorced in North Kingston, no kids, a croupier at Foxwoods, into huge earrings, fake lashes and enough mascara to cover North and South

America. Neither of the daughters wanted anything to do anything with their mother. Neither ever answered their phones.

Sometimes it was more than Grace could do to pick up the telephone and even talk to Shelia, let alone try to pick up the pieces.

At least Grace had a job. A profession and a job. She had always worked and would always work. Despite her own idiot boyfriend and the chaos he brought into her life. Despite it all.

Her job. Nurse care manager. Organize the resources necessary to keep people on Medicaid and Medicare out of the hospital. Hospitals cost money. Lots and lots of money. Way more than it cost the state to pay Grace to be nice to people who are old, lonely, anxious and sick.

So that was what Grace did every day. Be a nurse. Be a nice nurse. Listen to the old, the lonely, the anxious and the sick. Try to organize their chaos. Try to keep them from dying from their bad choices, even if they kept doing the same stupid stuff over and over. Even if they themselves don't care if they live or die. Just keep them out of the hospital emergency room, and please try to keep them from spending so much of our money on what won't change anything and is as likely to make them sicker as it is to keep them from dying, at least today.

No one tells the stories of nurses, of housecleaners, the stories of dog walkers or teachers or receptionists or bank tellers, of the women who carry the world on their backs, Grace thought as she waited for Shelia to come to the door. Or not. There is no American Idol for the work most people do, no Olympics for taking out the trash or picking the kids up from school or emptying a bedpan or starting an IV. They have taken our work from us. No one sees us anymore. All people see are figure skaters and football players on TV. Young white women in slinky dresses and young gay men with short, moussed hair waiting for the American Idol judges to rule, looking towards God and praying that the judges will choose them – them! so that they can realize their dreams. Not us, though. No one picks us. No one looks at us. The rest of us, the people who go to work every day and make the world turn – we no longer exist.

I've made plenty of bad choices of my own, one after the next, Grace thought, but at least not this bad. Yet. Still, there but for fortune.... Not that anyone else's choices have better results. You do what you gotta do and disregard the rest. You take one day at a time.

Shelia wasn't coming to the door. Do I call 911? Grace wondered. Do I get a cop to break down Sheila's door?

Grace had been to lectures about medical ethics. She remembered the principles, just words, really, words that kept banging around in her brain. Autonomy, beneficence, non-malfeasance, and justice. What does that all mean? Some professor's words. No help whatsoever. Another white male doctor with big ideas and no sense, who couldn't see what was right in front of his own eyes. Autonomy, beneficence, non-malfeasance, and justice. Not a chance. You take care of the people who need taking care of and listen when your heart speaks, even when you heart is talking trash.

Not how Shelia thought about the world, though. Good old Shelia. She just keeps on keeping on, putting one foot in front of the next, one cigarette or pain pill at a time, content as long as she can watch her soap operas on TV and have frozen pizza for dinner.

Die in the car, not live in the car, Grace thought to herself, when she'd talked to Shelia not one half-hour before. She's going get herself evicted. Evicted from a two hundred dollar-a-month trailer and then die in that car. Because of a damned two-page form.

So Grace got in her own car — 1996 red Thunderbird convertible, GRACE1 license plates, fast and sleek — and she drove over to Shelia's trailer.

I don't care what Shelia thinks or what she wants, Grace thought. I'll drive her to DHS myself. You just don't let a seventy-two-year-old with lung cancer get evicted and die in her car, alone on the street in the winter.

Shelia heard the banging on her door but she just didn't want to get up.

My back hurts, Shelia thought. I don't trust them social workers, I don't trust them nurses, and Rodney has the car. Rodney's at Foxwoods. Let them evict me, Shelia said on the phone when that nurse care manager called her. I ain't going to DHS. I ain't going to Roosevelt Avenue. I'd rather die in my car.

That nurse never gets me what I need, Shelia thought. Miss high and mighty. Don't like Rodney. Don't like me smoking. Drives the fancy car with them fancy license plates. Doesn't get me enough of my medicine. Rodney takes the medicine, and then what am I supposed to do? She don't know how much my damn back hurts. Hurts to move and hurts to breathe. That cancer is all in my bones. All my bones. Hurts all the time.

She heard more banging. It's the damned nurse, Shelia thought. I told her not to come. She come anyway, uninvited. UN-IN-VITED. The trailer is my goddamn problem. Not hers. Nobody lives forever. I'd ruther have my cigarettes and my pain pills than any old trailer anyhow. There's mold in this trailer, and it stinks down near the shower. Something must have died under there. Trailer's worthless, just like me.

Nobody's ever gonna come and fix it. Nobody's ever gonna come and fix the ceiling in the kitchen where the water got in. Nobody's gonna come and fix the hot water in the bathroom faucet, which comes out no better than an old man come to tinkle. Need the money for cigarettes. Rather live in the car then give them up. Who cares about some old trailer nobody can fix anyway?

When Shelia didn't come to the door, Grace thought, she's lying in there unconscious or dead. They had talked on the phone. Shelia knew Grace was coming. She could have taken too many Percocets – but she said she didn't have any Percocets. She could have fallen in the trailer. She could have hung up the phone and then just died, right there on the floor, purple as a violet.

If Shelia *was* in there, and just didn't want to open the door, what then?

What if she does get evicted? If that's what she wants, isn't it her choice. Isn't it her right to live on the street? What if she dies? But everyone with lung cancer dies, more or less. To die without even trying chemo, just because that leech of a boyfriend keeps taking the car to Foxwoods? The chemotherapy might give her a couple of more months. Might also kill her quick. One choice was worse than the next.

Grace's cell phone rang. It was her own damn boyfriend, that 250-pound asshole, calling again. Her leech of a boyfriend, or boyfriend only when he was in the mood, when some other woman had kicked him out because he was too much to bear. Her bad choice. One of many.

She let the call go to voicemail.

If Grace called the police and they broke the door down and Shelia was inside and just didn't want to talk to her, then what? If Shelia just didn't want to go to DHS and get the emergency rent money, wasn't that Shelia's choice? But if Grace called the police Shelia would probably never talk to her again, and whatever relationship Grace had carefully and slowly built with her would be for nothing — and Shelia would be even more stuck — no money, no chemo, no meds, Shelia on the street. If Shelia was lying unconscious on the floor, and if Grace didn't call the police, then Shelia would probably die, and it would all be for nothing just the same — no money, no chemo, no meds and Shelia dead. Shelia was going to die anyway, something no money, no chemo and no meds could prevent. Grace too. Everybody. It was just about when, and how, and with how much or how little suffering. About how much loneliness, fear and pain. Or about how much company Shelia or anyone else could stand. Some people die surrounded by people who love them. But not Shelia, not this time around.

Grace knocked again, longer and louder this time.

No answer. Inside, there were loud voices and music in the background. The blinds on the windows were drawn, but Grace could see flickering blue light reflected off the edges of each of the slats of the closed white mini-blinds. The television was on. Grace remembered that television. It was a big flat panel, about half the width of the trailer.

Grace took out her cell phone and called Shelia one more time. No answer.
Then she knocked again. Louder.
"Shelia, you ok in there? If you don't answer, I'm going to have to call the police, so they can come and check on you. You don't have to come to the door. Just tell me you are okay," Grace said, her voice loud enough to be heard across the street.

No answer.

Autonomy, beneficence, non-malfeasance, and justice.

As she entered the second "1" of 911, before she hit send, a car pulled up. Its driver hit the horn and Grace dropped her cell phone.

It was Rodney, in the beat-up yellow Dodge Avenger.

Shelia was sitting on a tired olive-green couch with wooden armrests that the varnish was worn from, in front of a TV which seemed three times her size, in a yellow and blue flowered housecoat, with her hair in curlers, a white kerchief with red flowers over the curlers, her eyes closed, holding a cigarette between the second and third fingers of her right hand, the cigarette burning into a thin dull off-orange colored metallic ashtray set on the couch in front of her. Her skin, which was more grey than pale, appeared blue in the constantly changing light from the television. A reality show was on, a show about police making arrests at night of women and men dealing drugs and involved with prostitution, their faces erased by the miracle of video technology.

The air in the trailer was thick and moist even though there was an air conditioner running. The trailer smelled of cigarette smoke, mold, and too much pine-scented air freshener.

"Turn it OFF" Rodney yelled, as they came in, and he slammed the front door.

Rodney was about five nine and covered with tattoos. He had slicked-back thinning grey hair, pink-tinted, black-rimmed glasses, a two-day beard, jowls, a loose fleshy neck that made him look older than he was, and red watery eyes. He was wearing a worn black leather jacket and had a metal chain that went from his waist midway down his thigh back to his side pocket.

Shelia half-opened, and then closed her eyes.

"YOU GONNA BURN THIS PLACE DOWN WITH THEM GODDAMN CIGARETTES," Rodney shouted. He walked to the couch, yanked the remote out of Shelia's left hand and stabbed at it.

Shelia shifted as though she were turning over in bed. The ashtray turned over onto the floor. The television went dark. The room seemed to shrink to just a fraction of the size it had been moments before.

Rodney leaned over Shelia, lifted her right hand with the care a violinist uses lifting her bow before the first note of a sonata, and with the two fingers of his right hand pinched the still burning cigarette from between the second and third fingers of Shelia's right hand. He placed Shelia's hand on the couch and stepped over her so he could open the bathroom door and flick the cigarette into the toilet bowl.

"Damn cigarettes," Rodney said from the bathroom, his back to Grace and Shelia. "She *is* going to burn the place down, that woman."

"Rodney!" Shelia said. "Where's.... my... *smoke*?" Shelia's eyes opened for the first time, and she sat up.

"Better this way," Rodney said.

Shelia fell back into her slumber.

Grace put the brown cardboard folder in which she kept each client's paperwork on the kitchen table and walked from the kitchen to the living room.

"Nurse is here," said Rodney.

"*Care* manager," said Shelia, her eyes closed, still slurring her words.

Shelia tried to sit up but fell to the floor.

"I'm calling rescue," Grace said.

The medical facts of the case were as follows. 72-year-old smoker with no hypoxic drive, likely having taken too much narcotic analgesia, with underlying pulmonary compromise secondary to metastatic lung cancer. Too many cigarettes. Too much opiate pain killer. No absolute determination to beat this thing, this cancer. A lifetime of bad choices.

Shelia's body was forgetting how to breathe. There was carbon dioxide building up in her blood, which was making her sleepy. The Percocet and Oxycontin were likely to make her quit breathing all together before long. Shelia needed a breathing machine. She needed to go to the emergency room and stay in the hospital to keep her breathing long enough until the Percocets and the Oxycontins wore off.

Rodney spun on his heels.

"She won't go," he said, as he slipped his arm under Shelia's neck. "She don't want no hospitals. No more."

"I don't DO hospitals." Shelia said.

"I got her." Rodney said.

Rodney lifted Sheila off the floor and laid her back on the couch. He lifted her feet onto the torn tan hassock that was in front of the couch. He brought a pillow and a blanket from the bedroom, which was at the far end of the trailer, to cover her.

Shelia's going to get evicted at the end of the week if I can't get her over to Roosevelt Avenue, Grace thought. She's going to die if I don't call rescue. She's probably going to die if I do call rescue. She's going live out her last days in that car or on the street. All she wants is a cigarette and then to be left alone to die in peace.

Grace's cell phone rang again. She looked at the number. That idiot again. His needs. His wants. His bullshit.

So Grace threw her cell phone against the wall with all her might.

The cell phone hit the wall in the kitchen with a thud and exploded into a thousand pieces. The thin walls of the trailer and the thin ceiling shook.

Rodney looked up and shrank back further into his tired yellow skin.

Shelia opened her eyes, took a deep breath, and sat up, still dazed. Then she closed her eyes and felt around her with her hands, looking for her smokes and a lighter, which she found on the floor next to her. Her hands shook as she took a cigarette from the pack. They shook as she put the cigarette in her mouth.

She spun the wheel of the lighter, her eyes still closed. She spun it once, twice, three times. The lighter caught. It produced a blue and yellow flame which burned above Shelia's thumb as she moved her hand toward the cigarette in her mouth, her hand swaying, see-sawing back and forth in the air.

Autonomy, beneficence, non-malfeasance, and justice.

Grace caught Shelia's arm in midair. She brought the hand and the lighter to the cigarette and held it there.

"Breathe," Grace said. "Inhale. Open your eyes."

Shelia opened her eyes a crack, just enough to see someone standing over her, holding her hand next to her smoke. She took a deep drag, long and slow but deep enough to get her cigarette lit. She took her finger off the lighter button and let her hand fall to her side. The cigarette hung from her bottom lip.

Then she exhaled.

And then Shelia inhaled again, the end of the lit cigarette glowing orange in the blue-white fluorescent light, orange like the sun at dawn.

Or sunset.

Job Lots

The big white man with the bad back put on a brown watch cap and his camouflage hunting jacket and took the nine guns from the locked grey metal gun cabinet that stood in the bedroom of the double-wide. An Anschutz Model 1710 D 22 Gauge rifle with a Kahles 2-7 x 36 mm rim-fire scope, a .50-caliber black powder muzzleloader, a Traditions .50-caliber shotgun with scope, a 12-gauge semiautomatic Remington 1100 shotgun, a 12-gauge Browning over-and-under, a New England Firearms 28-gauge shotgun, a 1858 New Army stainless steel .44 Caliper black powder revolver, a black powder Buckskinner pistol, and a Colt SAA 357 Magnum NKL revolver with a 5.5-inch barrel. Carl put them all in the back of the black Ford Explorer except for the 22 which he put on his lap and the Colt which he shoved next to his seat, wedged between the seat and the padded grey center console. Then he went back in the house for two green ammo boxes, one for standard ammunition, one for powder, patches, and balls. Black powder isn't much good for what would come next, but Carl wanted the three black powder weapons anyway.

He had nine guns with him, but you never know what you are really going to need to get the job done right. She did this shit to him over and over again. You turn your back one time and the bitch is at it again.

Don unpacked the carton. It was a carton of boxed citronella candles — yellow wax surrounding a thick white wick set in an ochre terracotta bowl that had been glazed olive green on the outside. The candles came one to a small tan cardboard box. The boxed candles were packed in pale brown cardboard cartons. The candles came a gross — a hundred and forty-four pieces — to the carton: four across, six back, six high. Don's job was to unpack the carton and place the candles in their boxes on the shelf in the seasonal section. The shelf was too narrow to hold more than three boxed candles front to back. Don made a row of eight candles that was three high. Three, front to back, eight across, three high. Seventy-two boxes. Half the carton. The rest of the carton would go back into the storeroom. It was late February, and no one would be buying citronella candles yet, but this was deep discounting – they bought up leftover merchandise, out of season or water-damaged lots or goods at bankruptcy sales, what people in the trade called job lots – and put the merchandise out there at low prices for bargain hunters. The store had the candles and the shelf space, and they wanted the candles unpacked. Don did what he was told.

When they told him they didn't need him anymore at Brown Price & Chase, Don hadn't been surprised or even saddened. He was sixty and tired. You could read the writing on the wall. It was 2009. The economy had tanked. No one was hiring executives – they were laying off executives left and right. There were search engines and social networking sites and websites for job searches. Hell, there were even websites for dating that did a good job. He was okay with the internet, and okay with Word, but his Excel skills weren't overwhelming. The young kids could make Excel jump into the air and do somersaults before he could even ask it a question using Help.

When you got right down to it, they'd never really needed him to do executive searches. Oh, he screened out the turkeys pretty well, the people who didn't really stand a chance in one particular job, who were over-reaching. But it really didn't matter who got what job beyond that because it was never clear what all the people Don recruited did, anyway. They went to meetings and wrote reports, meetings at which nothing much was decided, and reports that rarely drew any meaningful conclusions. So, finding one guy or woman who was particularly good at going to meetings and writing reports for a business or industry that needed people just to go to meetings and write reports was no particular challenge, and had not brought Don any particular joy. Paid the bills though.

Brown Price & Chase had been good to him. They kept him on for sixth months after the stroke. But fair was fair. His brain was fried. He couldn't really be an executive recruiter anymore.

The stroke took him out of work three months. It was way more than a stroke. Don nearly died. An infection on the artificial heart valve. A blood clot on top of the infection. Then the clot broke off in pieces and went to his brain and his spleen and his liver – even to his fingers and toes — where the pieces of clot showed up as little dark blue spots. Those clots gave him a stroke, or strokes, which meant he couldn't speak right and he couldn't always understand what people were saying to him, even though he could hear them loud and clear. Made his brain look like Swiss cheese on the CT scan. Made it feel like Swiss cheese when he tried to talk or think.

The work at Job Lot was okay work. Helped pass the time. He couldn't talk right and he didn't understand everything and his left arm was weak but damn it to hell he could do what he was told.

The candles done, Don carried the half empty box back to the storeroom and started on the seeds, doing it just like he had been told to. Build the display. Then put the seeds inside, one kind in each of the little boxes.

He brought all the materials for the seed display back to the Seasonal aisle. First, to build the display, there was lots of folding and pushing cardboard flaps around, but once you figured out the first part, the second, third and fourth part were easy, and all you had to do was do over what you'd done in the first part. Then the seed packets went into the display in alphabetical order.

He did the vegetable seeds first, then the flower seeds, which had pictures of the flowers on the front of the packets. Man, some of those flowers were pretty, asters and allium and bachelor's buttons, coreopsis, and daisies, echinacea and flax, galatia and hollyhocks, lupine, marigold and 5 different varieties of morning glory; nasturtium, oh, beautiful, edible nasturtium, phlox and poppy, rudbeckia, which he knew as black-eyed susan growing near the road, and six different sunflowers, sweet pea, verbena, yarrow and zinnias all lined up, one after the next in the cardboard stand. He could see each flower bending into the breeze, and he could taste the scent of half of them. In those flowers he could taste the sweet air of May, a taste that made him long to stretch out under a tree, read the morning paper or a book, and doze in the sunshine for a little while.

That was when he heard it. Voices that were loud and high pitched. More than one.

Running footsteps.

There was a man wearing a watch cap and an old army jacket standing between the checkout counter and the front window. The man's chest was crisscrossed by ammunition belts. He was holding a gun in each hand like some Mexican bandito, pointing one gun at the floor. A whiff of smoke came from that gun's barrel. It took Don a few seconds to find the sound of the shots that had just been fired in his memory. Gunshots! Holy cow! That guy was shooting! It took Don another half second to duck out of sight.

"Where is that bitch?" yelled the man in the watch cap. "And that asshole?"

Carl spun on his heels to where the other cashier was crouched under the second checkout counter. He fired again. He shot the tall white man with the crew-cut who was standing in front of the checkout counter paying for motor oil. Then he shot a short Hispanic woman in a black top and tight jeans who was next in line holding the hand of a five-year-old boy. The boy looked dazed as his mother, who also looked dazed, fell to her knees and slumped over, her hand pulling out of her son's hand as she fell.

"Where is that bitch?" Carl hissed, his teeth clenched. He squinted and paused for a moment. That bitch wasn't going to come to him when he called. Again.

Carl stomped to the other side of the third checkout counter, which was closed, and walked into the cookie and biscuit aisle, where they also kept the jams and jellies that were on sale.

Don, kneeling beside the garden supplies and seasonal merchandise, tried some quick thinking although he was not that good at thinking now. They sure didn't sell guns, knives, or even machetes in Job Lots. Rakes and shovels? Bungee Cords? Light bulbs? Tarps? Wrenches and screwdrivers? None of that was much good in an emergency like this. Maybe there was something he could use in the tiny hardware section in the back of the store, next to greeting cards. They had a couple of left-over splitting mauls on sale. Twenty-five percent off. A pretty good price. Or a hammer. Don could throw a hammer. If he could work his way back to Hardware and grab a hammer, he could get a jump on the shooter as the shooter walked down one of the aisles.

The five-year-old standing next to his mother dead on the floor started to whimper.

The bitch flunked out of nursing school, and now this, Carl thought. Nothing is ever good enough for her. She works nights in the nursing home, days over here, and now this. There's never supper on the table. She can't do the goddamned laundry. She can't sweep the goddamned floor. And now this. And the asshole stock boy? Tattoos and a pierced tongue? Nineteen fucking years old? *She* has a 17-year-old son! She gonna fuck him too? What's left? *She* wanted Carl to work late so they could have the above-ground. *She* wanted Carl to work late so they could have the hot tub, and *she* wanted Carl to work on weekends so she can get an SUV.

And now this.

Fuck her.

He reloaded.

The bitch wasn't in the pasta aisle.

There was an old lady with hearing aids and a walker in the towel aisle. Popped her.

There wasn't anyone in the kitchen utensil aisle.

Carl worked his way to the back of the store.

The bitch was too stupid to log off her fucking Yahoo account, so it was all sitting there, looking at him in the face when he got up in the morning and turned on the computer. The pictures of that stock-boy and his tattoos. Of her and her tattoos. Of the two of them together. Carl could still see those tattoos and that stock-boy's goddamned pierced tongue. If you don't log out, your email comes up automatically when you open your browser. Everyone knows that.

There was a sixteen-year-old tramp in a halter top trying to hide in the quilt aisle. He saw her foot out of the corner of his eye. He stamped down the aisle and caught her trying to slip into the greeting card aisle.

Popped her.

The bitch wasn't in the Greeting Cards either. Some old woman was. Last year's Valentine's Day cards were seventy percent off. Popped her.

The bitch was probably in the fucking stockroom.

Don found a nine-pound maul, heavy enough to split a log. He probably should have just picked up a hammer but then he thought the hammer might miss. The maul would bust open the guy's skull. One good swing. The maul was hard for Don to lift and would be hard to throw but the maul looked like it could do the job.

The kid in the front of the store was whimpering.

A male voice groaned.

Someone else was gurgling.

The Musak played *Want Somebody to Love* sung by a country and western singer, not Gracie Slick. There wasn't any other sound, though. You could actually hear the spitting and hissing of the fluorescent lights.

The shooter came out of Greeting Cards. He walked past Auto Supplies to Garden Tools, where the door to the stockroom was. Don lifted the splitting maul over his head. I'll smash his head as he is going into the stockroom, Don thought. I'll take him by surprise. While his back is turned.

Carl heard someone panting behind him. He spun around.

Just some old man struggling to hold a splitting maul over his head, his arms shaking. Carl popped the old guy too.

The bitch and the tattooed stock-boy were in the stockroom after all, and he popped them together.

Then he popped himself. No reason to stay and suffer. Live free or die. Time was up.

Donna could barely stand when she came to identify the body. Her sister Karen held her up. They looked like twins, Donna and Karen, though Donna was older and had been married once before.

Don was in the morgue.

The five-year-old had survived the whole thing. That child had been left standing there as that madness swirled around him. You had to feel for that child. What he had gone through. What he'd always remember. Growing up without a mother.

Don was in a bank of drawers, eight across, three high. He was in a middle drawer. Twenty-four drawers.

They found him easily enough.

Middle drawer. Three drawers from the right.

Isaiah on Route 6

At least she was wearing a mask. Covid-19. That was the only normal thing about the woman.

She appeared out of nowhere, in front of the old motel, near Cindy's Diner, across the street from the IGA Plaza where the Chinese restaurant is. Where Walgreens is. Which used to be Rite Aid which used to be Brooks Drugs which used to be Gregg's Pharmacy. Across the street from the gas station where they fill up propane tanks. Down the street from the hardware store.

She was almost six feet tall. She was walking on the side of the road toward Johnston and Providence. She had this great strong stride – nothing shy or contained about *this* woman. She walked with purpose. She wasn't mumbling to herself, spitting, shouting, or looking from side to side at unseen voices or at people she could see and hear but who weren't there. Dreadlocks, to be sure, but neat dreadlocks. Her face was smudged with something dark and grey, almost like war-paint, that looked like it had been put there by design. She did not look like a woman who had been sleeping in the woods, let me tell you. She was pretty well put together.

But the way she was dressed, man, that didn't make any sense at all. Some kind of shapeless brown cloth over her. It almost looked like she was wearing a burlap bag, the old sacks they used to pack coffee or feed in – but who has even seen a burlap bag in like, thirty years?

There's no law against walking on the side of the road. No reason to stop her. In the time of Covid, you don't want to go near anybody. Six feet apart, right? She wasn't breaking the law and she wasn't obviously crazy or hallucinating or a danger to herself or others. She just looked a little weird, walking like that. No one walks in America now. People hike, sure, with hiking boots and day packs or those fancy water sacs on their back which have tubes sticking out and with hi-tech walking sticks, one in each hand that makes it look like they are rowing, not walking. Or people bike the back roads on $10,000 bicycles made from space age materials wearing spandex biking shorts. But no one ever walks to get from place to place now. People drive when they have some place to go. That's just the way it is. Life in 2021.

Nobody called it in. Probably no one else noticed. Or even saw her. You don't even see what you've never seen before, most of the time, even if it's right in front of you. Like that old story of the Fuegians and Magellan's ships. They say that the Fuegians, the native people who lived on the southern-most tip of South America, couldn't see Magellan's ships when he sailed around Cape Horn, even though those ships were anchored right offshore. The Fuegians didn't know what ships were, how ships were made or what they do. Those ships were so far from the Fuegians' experience that the ships had no meaning to the Fuegians – so the Fuegians didn't even see them. We see only what we already know.

So no one besides me noticed her. Live and let live, I said to myself. But let me check on her once in a while. Make sure she's safe. That everyone is safe. Black lives matter and all that. Law abiding citizen. No need for any confrontation. Or trouble. I didn't want to make trouble for her. And I didn't want her making any trouble for me.

The state cop drove back and forth as I walked down Route 6. I stayed off the road, so there wasn't any reason to stop or arrest me. Not that cops ever need a reason to stop one of *us*. I was not afraid. Deep in my heart and so forth. Didn't want to get shot in the back though. Getting arrested wouldn't have been terrible but it was beside the point. Sitting in some jail cell in Scituate or Johnston or ending up at Intake at the ACI wasn't going to do anyone any good. The modern version of getting swallowed by a whale. But I didn't want to be out of sight, out of mind. I wanted to be seen. Acknowledged. Recognized. I wanted to be right there in the open. Unavoidable. Undeniable. I wanted people to see me, feel confused, be freaked out and start thinking.

It's not just racism, you know. There's plenty of that in the good old USA. Way too much. But racism is the symptom of a deeper much more dangerous disease. The disease is greed. Greed, arrogance, materialism, jealousy, lust, it's all in the mix. Narcissism. Only I matter. Only what I want counts. Only what I see and feel exists. We talk ourselves into little boxes from which we never emerge. People driving by might see a Black woman with dreadlocks walking on Route 6. But they don't see the sackcloth and ashes. Or think about repentance. And never look at themselves, never think that our wants and our choices are the cause of this pandemic and the rest of this empty mess, the stupid lives we have chosen for ourselves and one another. Buy now. Pay later. Dirt can't hide from intensified Tide.

The cars whiz past on Route 6, but the people inside them don't see *me* at all. Most of what they see are other cars, while their radios play Spotify, NPR or WPRO. Maybe they see a crazed homeless Black woman because everyone walking must be homeless, right? Maybe they roll up their windows, so they don't get panhandled when they stop at the light near the liquor store, or at the light in front of the gas station across the street from Bishop's Hill Tavern, or at the light at the pool store and Cumberland Farms, just past where the old Subway and the old fire-station used to be.

Let the oppressed go free. Feed the hungry. Bring the homeless into thine own house. Cover the naked. Thou shall not hide thyself from thy fellow human. Care for the widow and the orphan. Let justice well up as the waters, and righteousness as a mighty stream. Etc. Etc. You know the drill. We got plagues again now, Covid and what not. Black people getting shot in the back by police. Riots in the cities. Climate change with its floods and fires. Swarms of locusts in Africa, the whole nine yards. You think anybody in America would ever roll down the windows of their cars, turn off their car stereos, and ask me what I'm doing, decked out in sackcloth and ashes, walking down Route 6? Or think for one second about what is going on in this crazy world we've built where people can't be in the same room together anymore?

I crossed over into Johnston. Walked down that strip across from Cumberland Farms where the pool store is. Walked past the tire place, the auto parts store, Tractor Supply, Dunkin' Donuts and the Dollar Store.

It was late in the morning by then. The trees around the reservoir were red and gold. The air was filled with falling leaves and smelled of overripe grapes, maple leaves, diesel exhaust and wood smoke. You don't really live unless you walk in the fall air. You live and you feel and you breathe deep when you walk. Mine eyes were seeing the glory of the coming of the Lord, right here and now in Johnston RI.

You might think the Johnston cops would have noticed – you know how *they* are. But nothing. Nobody even slowed down to gawk. Just that state cop, who drove by every couple of minutes.

I wasn't expecting the guy at the house near the reservoir. The houses there are on a narrow strip of land between the road and the water. No sidewalk. That woman had to walk on the lawns and driveways, with only mailboxes between her and the whizzing cars, which all do 55 in a 30-mph zone. Just sayin.

Okay. There was a big flag flying from a huge flagpole in front of the house she was walking in front of. She was walking on their lawn.

The guy came barreling down the road in a big blue F350 with double rear tires and a swept-up exhaust that was pouring out black smoke. Two American flags, one on each side, snapped and fluttered in the wake of the truck, which coughed and bellowed and then quieted. It slowed where that woman was walking and then it turned into the driveway, right in front of her.

I didn't want trouble, but you always got to be ready. So I threw on my lights and swung the car around.

There are two lanes in each direction over there. My vehicle closed off one of those lanes. Pretty soon there was a backup of ten or fifteen cars. The cars slowed and people turned their heads to see what was going on, as if they had never seen a state police car with its light bar lit up.

The guy came out of his truck and ran right at her. No mask.

Holy shit, I thought. Here it comes.

"Stop," I yelled. My service revolver was pointed at the guy. I didn't think about it. It was just there.

But it was too late. The guy grabbed her before he heard me.

"Janine!" the big guy yelled. He was a big bear of a guy, six-two or six-three and three hundred pounds if he was an ounce.

"Dwayne!" she yelled back, and she wrapped him in a big bear hug.

Then they looked at me.

"You have a problem?" the woman said.

"You know each other?" I said.

"Like for a hundred years," the big guy said.

"We work together at the ACI," the woman said. 'I'm a psychologist."

"I run the auto shop in Industries. Teach the guys a trade."

I holstered my gun and shook my head.

Maybe there is a god after all.

Cancer

It made no sense. There was only one person on Elliot's mind that night despite all the people who had gathered. All Elliot could think of was Leslie and whether she would be in the house or not.

The whole band was there, the new guys and all the old guys. They'd come from all over the country, from all around the world. Phil came in from LA. Steve from Austin, Jack from Bali where he lived on the beach, drinking and hanging out, making tourist money from street music and gigs in bars. It was good to see those guys, and it filled Elliot's heart in an unexpected way. It made Elliot feel that his life was bigger than he thought, as if there was this huge part of himself that he didn't know was there.

The guys came, they played, and they were tight — note perfect, timing perfect, better than they had ever been. You wouldn't think the old guys and the new guys would mesh so well, know the music, know the timing, and give each other space, but there it was. One practice session and they had it down, the old stuff and the new stuff. Perfect. The old guys were respectful of the new guys and followed their lead; the new guys, conscious of the old guys and their skills, made space for everybody. Everyone played their piece. Even Jack behaved. Solid, hot, bluesy and soulful. Jack managed to keep a lid on his virtuoso lead guitarist shit, the stuff that blew everyone out of the water but didn't give his bandmates a moment to breathe. The music was note perfect. They were tight as a drum. They were together, playing for one another and for something bigger, playing in a way that made each of them feel way more than the sum of their parts.

And man, people came. They sold out The Urban three nights in a row. People Elliot hadn't seen in fifteen or twenty years came, along with his little clan of groupies, the people who showed up almost everywhere the band played. Schoolteachers. Nurses. Lawyers. Bureaucrats, truck drivers and mechanics, the women in slinky pickup tops and the men busting their asses to look like they didn't give a shit, in jeans and t-shirts, with baseball hats and watch caps. Some of the men had gained weight and looked pretty lame, dressed like that at the gig, even though they wore suits and ties for the day job. Some of the women had crossed over into looking old, their skin thick and blotchy, their clothing matronly, their graying hair short so they didn't have to bother with it anymore. It didn't matter. These were all Elliot's people. They had lived together and loved and cheated and were cheated on and played and danced and sang and died and lost friends and lovers, had kids and families and lost them or merged them along the way.

People came. The line to get in was out the door and up the block. Everyone danced and they all pretended together that nothing had or would ever change.

The Urban, in Pawtucket, their home venue in the old mill, was perfect. The staff asked no questions when they heard Elliot was sick. They just organized the benefit. Day and time. They lined up other bands to come and play. They put the benefit up on social media, so everybody in Providence, Worcester, Fall River and New Bedford knew. Hell, even the Boston people knew. And showed.

Elliot himself was on, really on. His voice and his timing were all there. He led like he always did, and everyone fell in behind him. Not an ego thing. Just the way it was. Pain under good control. It was there but he could ignore it. It was a fist just under his chest that had his innards in its grip and twisted them from time to time, like the fist was going to rip those innards out and drag his heart out with them. But his mind was on other things. He was in another place. The pain was there, but Eliot could put it in a box, in another room, so he could play and sing as if nothing else mattered.

The fist was how it started, the thing that Elliot would eventually come to call the cancer. The thing, the fist, the catch, the rock where there had never been a rock, started as a question – what's that, is something there? And then became a statement, then a paragraph and then it took over his brain and his life so that it was all he knew and all he felt. He dropped twenty pounds in a couple of weeks, so quickly he didn't notice it but everyone else did. They said he looked gaunt. Elliot was always a thin guy, thin and wiry, which is how you roll when you play guitar and spend half your life on stage, fronting this band and that. So no one ever said, Hey Elliot, you lost a little weight, looks good on you. No, all they said was, hey man, you okay? Elliot saw the questions and the fear in all their eyes, and finally admitted to himself that this was a thing.

Getting diagnosed and treated was tricky though. Elliot was a musician, by god. He lived all his life in second and third story walkups off Broadway and in Pawtucket or Cranston. Even lived for a little while in Central Falls. Once, he lived in a converted chicken coop in Foster. Musicians don't do health insurance. You live for the band, for the song, for the gig and for the contract. You hope for a girlfriend who has benefits. Some guys teach school or work as carpenters or even roofers by day. But that wasn't Elliot. In high school he played a little and thought he'd end up an accountant or lawyer and live in the white house with the picket fence in Barrington or someplace that specialized in white houses with picket fences. But then the music began to move, the bands jelled, fell apart and jelled again. Elliot wrote a couple of anthems that got everyone on their feet and everyone dancing, and then he couldn't put the music down. Locally famous. Toured in California, Texas, Georgia and New York. Clubs, not concerts, but always just on the cusp. And the music. The music was better than fucking in its own way. Fucking came with wanting, expectations, disappointments, hopes and rules. Music had some of that, to be sure, but you could always close the door, put on a pair of earphones, and just play. Or walk into a club where you're known, pick up a guitar and sit in. You find a place for yourself. And you can disappear into the beauty of the moment. Into harmony, which is everlasting.

So getting diagnosed was a struggle. What the hell is this? What do I do? I haven't had a doctor since I was a kid. I'm 57. My pediatrician retired thirty years ago. Both my parents are dead. Who the hell do I even ask?

He thought of calling Leslie then. But didn't. Couldn't. He didn't want to know where she was or with whom. He didn't want her to think he was sick. He just didn't want to think about it.

The musicians' union people knew a doctor who practiced out in the woods, a guy with whom they worked out some deal. Took Elliot two weeks to get in. The guy looked at him, heard the story, and started saying things like, do not pass go, do not collect two hundred dollars. He set up the blood tests and the CT scan and the MRI and made the connection to the cancer doctor, the oncologist. The cancer doctor grew up in Barrington and was the kid sister of one of Elliot's band mates in high school. She knew all about Elliot. Elliot was apparently some kind of hero to the people he had grown up with, the one person who stayed true to his calling, the one person who lived an authentic life. He had no idea. Lot of good all that was doing him now.

Chemo started. Radiation planned. The doctors presented him at their tumor board thing and argued about when and whether or not to do surgery. Spots on the lung ruled that baby out.

And the money. It was all crazy. They wanted more money than Elliot imagined existed on earth. Five thousand for this. Ten thousand for that. Twenty-five hundred every time he had chemo, not counting the medicines themselves which were eighteen and twenty thousand dollars a dose. Of course they never charge you in round numbers. They always charge you weird amounts, like $18,257.27, as if all the detail and decimal places make it okay that you have to pay for something that is only there to keep you alive, that makes it okay for someone to charge you to keep living at all.

Truth be told, Elliot didn't know where all the money was going to come from. They were never going to raise enough with three nights of benefit concerts at The Urban. The DVD would have to go viral, and that just wasn't happening. Forty years of playing in dive bars, playing good blues music and anthems that made people sit up and listen and then stand up and dance told Elliot that he had a lot but he just didn't have the special sauce you need to sell a million of this or ten million of that and earn him enough so he could move out to Malibu and get a house on a cliff overlooking the ocean. Not that he would have wanted to move if he'd hit it like that. These were his people. This was his place. His life.

The hospital people didn't seem to mind and Elliot himself didn't care about the money. They kept treating him and sending bills. He kept getting treated and paying little bits at a time. If and when he could. If and when his brain was clear enough of the drugs and the pain that he could write them little checks. Don't ask, don't tell, remember? He'd be gone soon enough. They could take his estate to court. His estate: one old car and ten sweet guitars. What a joke.

They went through a long set. The house was filled. Everyone was on their feet. People looked at Elliot with love and admiration. What could be better than that? You can't see the crowd when you're on stage, not really. Heads. Lights. Shapes. People dancing. You can't really see but you can feel the crowd, taste the energy. Faces get to be a blur. Lots of familiar faces. But not the one he wanted, not who he was looking for.

They took a break. Elliot walked through the crowd. People came up to him. They threw their arms around him, thanked him, blessed him, and touched him as he walked past. He made it look like he was going to the john. But nothing. She wasn't there. Wasn't coming. Wasn't coming back. Even now. He didn't want her back. All he wanted was to see her one more time.

Their last set was magic. As good as they were the first two nights, and as good as they were tonight, there was something different about that last set. All that love and longing, all the years and all their savage, disordered, dissipated, anarchistic integrity hit on that last set, which sounded more like a prayer than it did an anthem. We are one people. Free people. People who love and want to be loved just the way we are, the music said.

People were on their feet, but they stopped dancing. They just sang along, as if they were all lead singers, as if they all played guitar or all could blow on a sax until the music healed all wounds, until the boundaries that separated them completely dissolved.

Then he saw her. Leslie. She had come after all. She was standing in front of a pillar in the middle of the floor, stage right. She was standing alone, looking better than ever. But she was thirty feet away, with a guitar, a mike stand, a monitor, and fifty people between them, with the band in the middle of a song.

She looked better than ever, those clear blue eyes open to him and the world, her skin so clean it reminded Elliot of water. "You clean up pretty well," Elliot always said, back when they were together, whenever she dressed to go out. She had her hair up and she was wearing a blue, red, and gold silk scarf that made the room revolve around her, which made her stand out while everyone and everything else around her was a blur.

But she was thirty feet away, and not with him yet.

The band launched the last ballad, which was about Leslie, and Eliot sang it, right to her. He saw her lips move with his.

The problem when they were together was the way she disappeared, the way she lost herself in him. You can't dissolve yourself. It is always hiding somewhere, feeling denied or angry when you can't be yourself. It's a huge problem if you can't say and think what you want, feel what you feel, believe what you believe, and dream what you want to dream. He didn't do that to her. He swore he didn't. He wanted her to be herself, to be free, or that was what he believed. He loved her, and not himself. The problem was that she was afraid to be seen and she was afraid to love. And that he just didn't know how to love one person at a time, completely and unconditionally, and that he certainly didn't know how to love her.

Their last anthem was designed to leave the crowd on its feet. They weren't doing encores. That was the deal. Not this time. Go out with a blaze of glory, so this would be a night everyone remembered. Go into the streets, they sang. Take back our world. Stand up together. Stand up now.

She sang with him. She knew the words better than he did. She could have been on stage with him again. Should have been.

And then they were done. He pulled off his guitar. She was just thirty feet away.

But the crowd won't have it. They surged onto the stage. They stamped their feet and they kept singing. They touched Elliot's face and hands and neck. He tried to push through, to get to Leslie, but they lifted him off his feet, hoisting him on a chair high in the air as if he were a king or a bridegroom. The band joined in. They kept playing and the whole house sang together. One body. One place. One people. Even if just for a few minutes, late one Saturday night.

By the time the crowd put him down, Leslie was gone.

Perhaps she had never been there at all.

Soon he'd be gone as well.
The life he had chosen was full and rich.
But the life he wanted had slipped away.

From All Men

When Arthur Rubinow, the shamesh, the haysedonda of the Meeting Street Shul, counted the people in his mind, he found only six. Eight for Mincha/Maariv today. Six for Shacharit tomorrow. A minyan is ten. Ten men, once. Ten anyone, now. Ten Jews. He needed ten Jews to have a real service, ten people so that people saying Kaddish could mourn their dead correctly, with memory, honor and dignity, sing G-d's praises, read Torah and learn together.

They were a dwindling community, but they were a community nonetheless. Once upon a time, not so very long ago, the early morning minyan had been warm and vibrant. They davened in a chapel in the basement of the synagogue, a moldy place made of dark wood that faced east and which surrounded by stained glass windows that depicted blue and green leaves and kept out the light. Thirty men, even in the middle of summer, when families went to their beach houses for weeks at a time. Ten or fifteen women, who sat off to one side. There was never a wall or even a curtain between the men and the women. They were not a community that needed a wall. People just knew where to sit, and everyone respected everyone else.

Before, most of the men had come from Europe, most from before and some after the war. They worked in or ran businesses: a candy factory owner, a furrier, a dry cleaner, a junk dealer whose children would call him a recycler of used building material after they got into real estate, a furniture store owner, a couple of sales-clerks, a jeweler or two, a rug dealer, and the owner of the little department store owner in Central Falls whose father started as a peddler walking from place to place, carrying his wares on his back. The Hebrew teachers and the Jewish community people, the functionaries who ran the Federation and the JCC and HIAS and the Hebrew Free Loan fund, they came as well, but less often than you might think. They were American born, and didn't feel the pain of history and the sadness of unrequited longing in their souls the way the generation who had been born in the shtetl or in Warsaw or Budapest or Bucharest or Prague did.

The children of the daveners from Europe, the second generation, the doctors and lawyers and engineers, were different. Some came as children and continued to come, in smaller and smaller numbers after they grew up, but most didn't come at all. That generation didn't really know how to daven even though they could read the words. They used Sephardic trope—even though their families were from Eastern Europe—because that was the way Hebrew was spoken now, in what Arthur Rubinow always called the new state of Israel, even after Israel was 60 years old. The second generation came because their fathers came, out of respect and a little fear. Those who came were the ones who had respect and fear. Many of that generation and most of the generation which came after them had no respect for anything that had come before them. Most of them ran wild in the streets.

That older generation, the generation of immigrants, they really knew. They knew Torah, they knew Talmud, they knew how to daven, how to pray with their whole souls, and they had sachel, wisdom. They listened before speaking and they turned a problem or idea over in their minds, thinking out all the ramifications before answering a question or stating their beliefs. More often than not, they answered a question with a question. Who is a fool? the Pirkei Avot asks. He who knows not and knows not he knows not. Who is wise, the Pirkei Avot asks? And answers: he who learns from all men.

When the minyan was at its height, the Chapel would be full twice a day. Sometimes the late-comers, the people who lived in the suburbs and arrived a few minutes late or the men who stayed at business a little too long in the late afternoon, they would have to stand in the back. The late comers had to use cast-off siddurim, the old prayer books which had different page numbers and worn covers.

Each of the regulars had a seat, of course, and every man knew who would lead which part of the service at which time and on what day. On Mondays and Thursdays, when they read Torah, everyone knew who would get the first Aliyah and everyone knew that the last two, before and after the misheberach, the blessing for the sick, were reserved for guests or newcomers, so that even the young men, who often came trailed by a son or a daughter of four or six, had a job to do and a place in the community, so that everyone felt included and respected. Each man shook the hand of every other man after their part or after an Aliyah, so by the time the davening was finished, every man had shaken the hand of every other man in the community ten or twenty times. Yes, just the men. That was normal. Part of daily life, something no one even noticed or questioned but which happened every single day of the year, year in and year out.

But then generation from Europe began to die off. The doctors and lawyers and accountants came, but only once or twice a week, or only on shabbos, or only mornings or only evenings and gradually not at all. The minyan thinned. There was a moment in the late seventies and eighties when the Russians arrived, and it looked like the minyan might grow again. But the Russians didn't last. Their old men knew how to read but they didn't know Torah and Talmud, they didn't daven with their souls the way the old men born in Poland, Galicia, Romania and Lithuania did, and the Russian men didn't mix much with the rest of the minyan. The old Russian men died off quickly, and their second generation didn't come at all.

The minyan felt the loss of each man, of each person, the loss of the men who knew and their wives who came with them and sat off to the side. Each loss left a gap, a hole that could be felt and even seen, a lost tooth, because everyone in the minyan knew the voice of every other person, knew the way they would sing a certain part. What had been a robust and guttural chorus when the minyan sang or spoke the shema or the borachu or words or lines of the kaddish together, became a few voices, singing alone together, the women's voices clearly heard now, and sweet, because most of the few women could at least carry a tune.

Sometimes only fifteen or twenty men came. Then only twelve or thirteen. Many seats went unfilled. The chapel was renovated and moved from the basement to the top of a flight of stairs, facing south, not east, so the sun streamed through the windows at sunset in winter, and the old dark wooden benches were replaced by blond wood chairs with nice upholstery.

They coped. First the shamash and the gabbai were replaced by men who were American born. Then they started counting women to make the minyan, as the need for ten men became the need for ten people. Then women had Aliyahs and then women read from the Torah and then a woman became the gabbai. Who knew?

But despite all the change, the minyan shrank. Some days they waited fifteen or twenty minutes for a minyan. Some days thirty minutes. Some days an hour. Some days Arthur Rubinow called his friend Morty to come over to make ten. Some days he asked his wife Diane. They thought about and discussed opening the ark and counting the Holy Presence to help them get to ten people, as they did in some of the tiny communities in Galicia and Georgia, but then their Rabbi ruled against such a practice. There were enough Jews in the community to make a minyan. So the responsibility was to find more people to come. Was minyan attendance also the responsibility of the Holy One, Blessed be He? No! It was the responsibility of the community! But then the Rabbi himself didn't come any more, so what sense did any of it make?

Some days they didn't get ten people at all, so mourners couldn't say Kaddish, they couldn't read Torah, and they couldn't recite the Shemoneh Esrei out loud or say the Kaddusha at all.

There was a new minyan of hippies who met in the chapel on shabbos after the early morning minyan was over, and the two groups met on the stairs or coming through the doors. The men had long hair and the women had tattoos and piercings, like Canaanite harlots or the Moabite ritual prostitutes described in Bereshit. They drummed and played guitars. Young people. But at least they came to shul.

Now everything was different. Women rabbis. Cantors who were converts. Gay men and lesbians and people who went from one gender to the other and back. There were people of color in that minyan. Chinese people and people from India and Africa, people whose skin was as black as charcoal. The world had changed. The people of the early morning minyan barely recognized the new world they were in.

One shabbos in early summer, when some of the regulars were at the beach, when the sun was very strong even though it was early, only five people were sitting in the seats and only eight all together were coming. Two women. Three men. Five. Better than nothing. Still, Arthur Rubinow announced the page, and David Weinstein, a retired dentist, began the preliminary prayers. Everyone understood that Kaddish D'Rabbanan would be left out. People would trickle in, and some of those parts could be added back at the end of the service once they got to ten. If they got to ten. If a miracle happened.

But Arthur Rubinow had already counted in his mind, and he knew a minyan was impossible. Diane Berkovits was at the beach. The Golds were visiting their son and new daughter-in-law in Bethesda. The Aronowitzes were in the Berkshires. Arthur Kaplan had just had foot surgery and couldn't walk yet. Arthur Rubinow had made his phone calls the evening before and he knew what he knew. Eight. With luck they might get eight. But no more. The world was full of Jews but no more than eight Jews in the whole city were available to pray together, read Torah and sing G-d's praises that day in late June.

The door lock buzzed. There were footsteps on the stairs. Penelope Yellin came in and took her usual seat, so now they were six. They did not say Borachu but they read the Shema out loud together. You can say the Shema alone so you can certainly say it with only six.

Arthur Rubinow closed his eyes and went out into the hallway where he could use his cellphone without being seen. Pikuach nefesh. It is permissible to break all rules in order to preserve life. Wasn't a minyan life itself? He texted Morty and Diane. Diane texted back. She was getting out of bed and would drive over. That would make seven. Jeffery Sussman, their Gabbai, would arrive right at 8:17 as he did every shabbos, just in time for the Torah reading. He was a lawyer and acted like the rules that applied to everyone else didn't apply to him. But he came every week, and that was enough for them. They might get to eight. But no more. Ten was impossible, at least this week. They would cope, they would go on living, and G-d willing, they would have a minyan again shabbos the following week when people returned from their travels.

But a little part of Arthur Rubinow felt shame nonetheless. They were a community, and as a community they had failed to keep this small promise to themselves. He was a man, and he had failed to find ten people, in a world that was full of people, in a world that had once been full of men who wanted only to stand together, to sing G-d's praises, to remember, to give to charity, to do good deeds, and to carry on. Now there was almost nothing left. He had been delaying the inevitable and was unable to admit the truth. There just weren't enough people for a minyan anymore. He lived in a lost world.

They were ready to read the first Amidah. Waiting for more people wasn't going to change anything. The Amidah would have to be said silently, without the Kiddusha. Arthur Rubinow stood to announce the page.

But when Arthur Rubinow opened his mouth, a siren came out instead of words. An earsplitting, brilliantly painful, too-loud-to-think siren. WHHOP WHHOP WHHOP WHHOP. Who makes noises like this on shabbos? For a moment, Arthur Rubinow wondered if he was having a stroke, and perhaps the siren was only in his brain. But the other people looked around, put down their siddurim, their prayer books, took off their tallesim, folded them, put them on their seats, and marched toward the doors. The siren was a fire alarm, and it was LOUD.

Arthur Rubinow followed the little group out the door, climbed down the stairs, and left the building.

Three fire trucks pulled up in front of the shul, their red and white lights bathing the streets. Two police cars arrived, adding blue and white lights to the red and white lights washing the buildings and the cars. The street smelled like diesel exhaust, though there was still a hint of the sweet green taste of late spring because of all the flowers and trees that were in bloom in the plantings and from the trees planted next to the street.

Teams of firefighters went into the building. The six people from the minyan clustered on the sidewalk in front of the stoop. The men still all wore kippahs and the women wore white lace dollies pinned to their hair. The little knot of people standing together looked somehow out of place, six Jews in nice clothing standing together on a bright June morning as firemen with red fire hats and yellow rubber fireman's boots stood in front of their trucks, trotted back and forth to the shul, or prowled inside the synagogue.

"I didn't smell smoke," Pauline Yellin said.

"Was my davening that bad that it set off the fire alarm?" David Weinstein asked.

Diane walked down the sidewalk and joined them. Jeffery Sussman arrived. Now they were eight. Eight Jews on a sidewalk. Too few and with no place to go.

The firemen walked in and out. A team of three, carrying an oxygen tank, came out of the building. Better they are coming out than rushing in with hoses, Arthur Rubinow thought. In a real fire we would need to go in ourselves to rescue the Torahs, to protect them. Six Torahs in the chapel alone. Many more in the main sanctuary and the vault.

More firemen came out.

The fire trucks turned off their flashing lights. Then the police cars drove away.

False alarm, Arthur Rubinow thought. We'll go in soon and finish. Only eight of us. No Torah reading. We'll finish fast.

"How long do we wait?" David Weinstein said.

Arthur Rubinow approached a group of firefighters who stood in front of the first truck, killing time. Two smoked cigarettes.

"Gentlemen are we free to return to the building?' he said. "Fire, or false alarm?"

"No false alarms, only tests of systems integrity," one of the firefighters said. His hat was under his arm. He had a ruddy complexion, a thinning hairline, and a bushy moustache.

"No fire. If there was a fire we wouldn't be standing here, blowing smoke," said a second firefighter, who was tall, dark skinned and powerfully built.

"Ya gotta wait for the Fire Marshall to sing," said a young one, who was fair and pale, slight but with big shoulders and blue and green tattoos that flowed over his arms and neck and had close cropped red hair and green eyes. "They check carefully. I think he's almost done. Hey, Shabbat Shalom, Mr. Rubinow, it's Neil Green."

Arthur Rubinow took half a step backward. Neil Green was a little boy, a mischief maker, a pipsqueak, who came to shul only once in a blue moon, when his divorced father, an animator for a film studio, was in town and came to say Kaddish. The mother was a teacher and was Portuguese. She had converted when the kid was born, but lost interest as soon as the father moved out. Neil Green. He was a kid Arthur Rubinow always gave candy to when he came to shul so his memories of Torah would always be sweet. Who knew?

"No hurry," Arthur Rubinow said. "We're only eight. We'll be done in five minutes."

Two men in orange hats came out of a side door. They were older guys, in their forties or early fifties, ruddy faced and beefy.

"All clear," one of them said. "You can go back now."

We'll have to hurry, Arthur Rubinow thought. We started twenty minutes late. We davened for ten or fifteen minutes before the fire alarm and have been twenty or thirty minutes outside. The hippies with their drumming will be here before long. Start on Page 115. It shouldn't take us long.

The others were starting to go inside.

A young man wearing a kippah and carrying a tallis bag walked toward the shul. Or perhaps it was not a young man. The person walking had long hair that was held in place by a hairband, and glasses, and wore a white shirt and trousers. One of the hippies coming to drum, a little early.

"Shabbat Shalom," the person said, and held the door for Arthur Rubinow.

"Shabbat Shalom," Arthur Rubinow replied. "Can you daven with us? We don't have a minyan yet. We'll be done in five minutes."

"Of course," the person said.

They walked up the stairs together, both of them. One more person. A little closer to a minyan, and perhaps a little closer to G-d.

Then the buzzer went off. Someone was at the locked door. It was one of the firemen. Neil Green. Arthur Rubinow went down the stairs to let him in.

"I can stay until we get another call," Neil Green said. "The boys on the truck'll wait. Capt'n's good with it."

Arthur Rubinow and Neil Green, this pipsqueak, now a man, also walked up the stairs together, also both of them.

They had ten. Ten including two people neither Arthur Rubinow nor any of the other regulars even knew existed. They were a community, however thrown together by accident, however worn out, accidental and ragtag, and together they could daven together, remember the past, mourn the dead, and learn.

The world had changed under their feet while the people of the early morning minyan weren't looking. Neither better nor worse. Just different.

What is holy? G-d is holy. Kindness is holy. Justice is holy. Who is wise? He, and now she, and now they, who learn from all men. And women. And everything and everyone else in between.

21 Horses

A heavy white woman with a bad right knee pulled herself up the steps of the #99 North Main Street bus at the very same moment twenty-one prized polo ponies, each worth more than $200,000, were dying at the International Polo Club in Wellington, Florida. The polo ponies were part of the Venezuelan Lechuza Caracas polo team and were about to compete in the prestigious U.S. Open Polo Tournament.

The heavy white woman had taken the #71 Bus from Broad Street in Central Falls and would transfer again at Kennedy Plaza. She taking the bus to see how long it would take, to see if it was something she could actually do with her knee hurting as much as it did. She would be back the next day to interview for a job at an after-school program in South Providence, teaching Hmong, Dominican, Honduran, Liberian, Bhutanese, Nepalese, Native American, Black, Cape Verdean and Puerto Rican kids how to sew.

In her mind, the job — teaching in an after-school program — would lead people to her website, and she would be able to sell all the needlepoint she had sewed, and that would lead to more orders than she could handle. She could see herself, as she slowly climbed the bus stairs, renting out loft space and hiring a hundred women like herself, women with children and quick fingers but no real chance of doing anything other than surviving. She could see herself building a business that would make her known the world over.

The bus driver, a thin, squirrelly, olive-skinned woman in her mid-forties, was in a hurry for this new passenger to make it up the stairs because she had a schedule to keep. The olive-skinned bus driver was in a hurry because she was always in trouble with her supervisors for being overly familiar with her passengers and for running far behind. The bus driver liked talking to the passengers. She gave her regular passengers nicknames, and sometimes sang to them as they climbed the bus steps.

"Take your time, sweetheart," the bus driver said, as the heavy white woman lifted her leg to the second step. The heavy white woman grasped the grab bar on the left side of the door, and pulled herself up with her arms, swinging her unbendable left leg out in order to get it over the edge of the second step.

"You need to win Powerball and get yourself a car, sweetheart," the bus driver said.

The heavy white woman was now out of breath.

"Don't...want... no... car," she said. "Just... want... to... get... up... these... blinking... steps."

The heavy white woman, still short of breath, showed her fare card and limped to a seat behind the driver, collapsing into it.

The last thing the heavy white woman wanted to talk about was Powerball or anything like a car. She had learned a long time ago not to want what could easily break and cost money. Most things that other people wanted were things that could break, things that cost money, things that all made trouble. That was true of people as well as things.

There were many things she didn't want, and many people she wanted nothing to do with.

What she did want, though, was a house, but that was more for her son than it was for herself. A simple house, just like other people have. Not a mansion. Not a castle. Just a house. Any place would do. Fairlawn or Darlington would do. Valley Falls or Ashton would be nicer, but there were lots of places that would be just fine – Oaklyn Beach, Artic, even West Warwick or Connimicut, though those places were five or ten miles away and felt like they were on the other side of the moon. One of the houses you see in the Saturday Journal – in the classifieds, not the house of the week. One floor. Heat that works. Water that works. It could be a rental, but a rental where the landlord wasn't going to sell the house out from under them after five months again, with a landlord who would actually come and fix what broke and make sure the garbage got picked up.

2.

On the grounds of the International Polo Club in Wellington, Florida, polo ponies valued at $200,000 each were being unloaded from sleek aluminum horse trailers onto the brilliant green paddocks of the Polo Club, paddocks which were surrounded by perfect white fences. Elegant young women in spring dresses made of boldly colored flower print fabric mingled with older women in pert hats and with well-groomed South American men in linen suits, sipping champagne.

3.

There weren't many people on the bus – perhaps ten in all, sprinkled around the seats — a teenaged Asian girl with blue hair, sitting about halfway back; a thin very dark young man in a pressed white suit; and an older man who was short and squat and was wearing a tan golf jacket, sitting a few seats behind the young man in the white suit. One or two other men and women sat in the rear of the bus — the women, sitting alone, doubled up shopping bags on their laps, looking vacantly in front of themselves; the men slumped over and sleeping. Two women speaking Cape Verdean Creole sat next to one another in the seats just behind the rear doors of the bus.

The bus traveled down Pawtucket Avenue, past Murphy's Liquors and Ocean State Job Lot, the big one next to the Laundromat that closed. Then it stopped across from Gregg's, next to where Sears used to be, just across the street from Midas Muffler and the place that sells motor scooters, the one with the red motor scooter up on the roof that they use as a sign.

4.

It was clear the horses in Wellington Florida were in trouble as soon as they were unloaded from the trailers. They were disoriented. They stumbled, shaking their heads, and shied away from their grooms. They pulled against their leads, coughing and blowing mucus and foam from their huge nostrils, their eyes rolled back and to the side as if they were being chased but had no place to hide.

Then they went down. People began running from one horse to the next, shouting directions and calling for help in the perfect warm afternoon.

5.

A man and a woman got on the bus.

The man was in his late thirties. He was wearing a cracked grey-brown leather jacket that was worn at the elbows and the collar. He had glazed hazel eyes that were almost green, slicked-back hair, and he needed a shave. The woman was pregnant. When she struggled to pull herself up the steps of the bus, the man put his hands on the woman's haunches and pushed, as if mocking the woman's pregnancy. He grinned. He knew everyone in the bus was looking them and that there was nothing anyone would do or say to stop him.

The pregnant woman was perhaps twenty-five. She had puffy brown skin and dirty brown hair that was pulled back and tied with a yellow elastic band behind her head. She was wearing a navy-blue sweatshirt with a hood and black spandex pants that clung to her protuberant belly, which she balanced by throwing her chest, shoulders, and buttocks backward, so she waddled when she walked.

6.

The polo team Lechuza Caracas was owned by Victor Vargas, a multimillionaire from Venezuela, a man who also owns a bank, three airplanes, two yachts, and six houses. Vargas, a man who said of himself that he "has always been rich," is from a wealthy Venezuelan family which has always been rich. Vargas's son-in-law is the great grandson of the Spanish fascist dictator Francisco Franco, who ruled Spain with an iron fist for 40 years.

7.

It had been a brilliant day. Mid-April. The sky had started out clear and blue, the air was crisp in the morning, and the light breeze from the southeast brought the clean, sweet, salty taste and smell of the ocean up from Narragansett Bay as that breeze blew away the oil smoke from house furnaces. That smoke left behind a residue that made the pastel nylon and aluminum siding of the houses look gray and tired. Now, in the middle of Sunday afternoon, clouds had moved in and the sky was dark but the air was still a little warm, for April; daffodils were up and the trees were budding but not yet in bloom.

The pregnant woman produced a wallet and put money in the fare meter. Then, with the same exhausted collapse with which the heavy white woman had thrown herself into a seat, the pregnant woman threw herself into a seat just across the aisle, just behind the bus driver but on the other side of the bus. Her consort, the man with slicked-back hair and hazel-to-green eyes, stood in front of her for an instant, looming over her, as if to make her remember that he owned her.

Then that man slumped to the floor.

He didn't get up.

He lay on the floor of the bus lifeless, and his face got gray, like the color of shirt cardboard.

There is always an instant of hesitation among onlookers when there is a sudden change in the status of people or events. We are so used to things as they are, as they have always been and as we expect them to be that we cannot believe our eyes when things change right in front of our eyes. We believe what we are used to believing, not what we see.

The bus pulled out onto North Main and was halfway up the block by the time the man hit the floor. The brown-skinned pregnant woman in the navy-blue sweatshirt watched the man fall out of the corner of her eye. She rarely ever looked right at him. H was just a man who had marched into and taken over her life. She'd never had any control over her life, and she didn't have the energy to throw him out. He was goofing, right? That man always had an angle.

The man with slicked-back hair and hazel-to-green eyes twisted as he fell, his right shoulder coming to rest on the row of hard green-blue fiberglass bus seats. His leg bent and twisted under him, and he hung like that for a few moments until the bus lurched forward. The movement of the bus sent his torso backwards, toward the rear of the bus. His shoulders slid to the floor of the bus. He landed on his side and his head hit the floor. There was no muscle tone in his body at all. It wasn't clear if he was breathing.

The heavy white woman with the limp watched him fall, unable to believe what she was seeing.

But by the time his shoulders were resting on the row of green-blue seats, the heavy white woman was on her feet.

"Hey" she said, loudly enough so that everyone in the bus could hear, know there was trouble, and know that the trouble was in the front of the bus.

Even the man at the back of the bus who had been sleeping with his head against the window sat up suddenly and then found himself on his feet.

8.

Over a hundred people in Wellington Florida came down from the stands to try to save the horses, and each horse had five or six people clustered around it, calling instructions, listening with stethoscopes, giving shots or holding IV bags. Some of those people used newspapers or a program to shield the horses' eyes from the sun. They kneeled next to each horse, patting its sweat-drenched neck.

9.

The heavy white woman found herself in motion.

The bus driver, sensing commotion behind her, started to pull the bus to the right so cars could pass. But then the bus driver panicked. She stopped the bus in the middle of the street. The bus driver stood up, turned, and put her hand over her mouth, hyperventilating.

The pregnant woman in the navy-blue sweatshirt slid away from the man on the floor and put her hands on both sides of her face, her eyes welling with tears. The man on the floor was not the father of her baby, but she didn't want *this* to happen. She was done with him, so done. But he was who she was with now. She didn't know what to do or what to say.

The heavy white woman found herself on the floor next to the man in the worn leather jacket with the slicked-back hair and hazel-to-green eyes, which now stared vacantly at the ceiling. His head flopped against his shoulder. His skin now looked ashen and almost yellow or green.

The heavy white woman found the man's right wrist, felt for a pulse and then looked at his face, which was completely motionless.

"Call 911," she said, loud and clear, not looking up.

Then the teenage Asian girl with blue streaked hair knelt next to the heavy white woman. The young Black man in the pressed white suit stood just behind the teenage Asian girl.

"Begin CPR," the heavy white woman said. The heavy white woman had no idea how to do CPR herself, and no idea of when CPR should be started or stopped, but she had seen people on TV doing CPR when other people collapsed and it was the only thing she could think of to say. She looked up and saw that the bus driver was still standing next to the steering wheel, her hand still over her mouth, and was still hyperventilating.

"Call 911. Now," the heavy white woman said. This time the bus driver leaned over her seat, picked up her radio, and called 911.

"Pump his chest," the heavy white woman said.

The heavy white woman put one hand under the left arm of the man in the worn leather jacket to move him onto his back, and suddenly there were ten hands under him, as everyone else in the bus was now crouching next to the heavy white woman. They lifted the man in the worn leather jacket together, and suddenly the man in the worn leather jacket was as light as a song. They laid him flat on his back.

Then the heavy white woman leaned over and put her mouth over his mouth. His mouth was cool, strangely dry and tasted of cigarette smoke and stomach acid, but somehow it tasted sweet nonetheless, like mint. Actually, his mouth tasted like an Icebreaker. The heavy white woman closed her eyes, and the huge breath that came out of her surprised her with its force. The man's chest rose, towering over where it had been, as if it had doubled in size.

10.

Thirteen horses died on the field at the International Polo Club. One horse was put down at the Palm Beach Equine Clinic. Seven horses died at the Lechuza Caracas barn before they could be loaded into the truck or moved to the veterinary clinic. There were tears in the eyes of Victor Vargas, a multimillionaire from Venezuela, owner of the polo team Lechuza Caracas, a man who also owns a bank, three airplanes, two yachts, and six houses, and whose son-in-law is the great grandson of the Spanish fascist dictator Francisco Franco, a man who ruled Spain with an iron fist for 40 years.

11.

Three police cars descended on the bus, one stopping just in front of it and two behind it, their emergency lights flashing blue, red and white. What little traffic there was slowed to a halt and then backed up to the old Shaw's Plaza where Gold's gym used to be and where LA Fitness is now. Rescue came. They took over CPR from the heavy white woman, the Asian girl with the blue streaked hair and the young black man in the pressed white suit, who had been taking turns pounding on the man's chest and breathing for him. Then Rescue scooped the man up, carried him off, and the incident was over as quickly as it had begun.

Everyone on the bus stood and looked at one another, and then looked away.

The bus driver made another call on her radio and then began talking about how nothing like that had ever happened on *her* bus to *her* passengers.

A few minutes later, a light blue car with yellow emergency roof-lights pulled up in front of the bus, and a woman in an olive uniform like the uniform the bus driver was wearing led the bus driver away. Another bus driver who had also come in the blue car climbed into the seat of the bus and spoke calmly over the bus PA system.

The brown skinned pregnant woman in the blue sweatshirt was crying and talking on her cell phone. She started talking to the new bus driver and was soon screeching at him. She kept screeching until one of the policemen came into the bus. The policeman helped the pregnant woman down the steps. She stopped screeching and sobbing as she got into one of the police cars that were parked at odd angles around the bus.

The police cars turned off their flashing lights.

As quickly as they had come together, the ten people who had clustered around the man in the worn leather coat and had been like one person, with one purpose, went back to their own lives. The young Black man in the white suit returned to his seat, shaking his head.

But the heavy white woman got off the bus, crossed the street, and stood at the bus stop that was in front of a pawn shop. All she wanted now was to be back home.

12.

It wasn't raining yet, but it soon would be. Suzanne Williams was still amazed by the force of the air that had come out of her mouth when she was doing CPR and by how cool and dry the man's mouth was.

Like the taste of mint. People had listened to her and followed her lead. Nothing like that had ever happened to her before.

As she stood there, waiting for a #99 bus to come north on North Main, just for an instant, she became many different people in her own mind, one after the next, each just for an instant: a tall, thin white woman in a business suit, wearing a string of pearls, sitting at a board table with other people wearing business clothes; a young brown-skinned woman with long pulled back hair, wearing a tee-shirt and a long skirt, standing in front of a microphone; an intense stocky olive skinned man in his thirties with slicked backed dark hair, calling out slogans to a crowd of 50,000 standing in front of the State House, a crowd that was on its feet with arms raised high, calling back to him; a thin, worn-out junkie with stringy hair and bad makeup, standing on a street corner under a streetlight on Broad Street in Olneyville. Then she became Suzanne Williams again, the Suzanne Williams who was standing on North Main Street, just waiting for the #99 bus.

Two days later, Suzanne Williams learned the man had died. His obituary ran six lines.

Just a picture and six lines. No details. As if he had never existed at all.

Woke

It wasn't hard for Crystal to get what she wanted because she didn't want very much. Crystal didn't want to be the boss. She didn't need much money. She was content with her lot. Nothing she ever tried that might change her life had ever improved it. But what was hers was hers, and all she wanted was for things to stay the way they were.

Jake was hired late one September to take over the organizing, and Jake was everything Crystal wasn't. Jake was 27, 6'4" and thin as a rail. He had dreadlocks and crème colored skin. Crystal was 58. She'd been through a liver transplant. Her skin had a grey tinge from the anti-rejection drugs; her face was puffy from the steroids. She kept her once brown hair short and plastered in place so it didn't get in her eyes and so she didn't have to mess with it all day, like the pretty girls with no substance who spent half their lives in front of a mirror. Even so it wasn't that long ago that Crystal herself wore her hair long and tied it behind her head so she could let it down when the wind blew or when she was just fed up with being polite.

They worked for a little non-profit in a storefront office.

The front window had a big picture of the Statue of Liberty, with the words, 'Give us your tired, your hungry and your poor' next to it, and then WELFARE RIGHTS. FIGHT FOR 15. HEALTH CARE

FOR ALL. FOOD STAMP ADVOCACY. ENVIROMENTAL JUS-
TICE POOR PEOPLES CAMPAIGN written in big letters across the
top, and big pictures of Martin Luther King, Mother Teresa, and John
Fitzgerald Kennedy in the window.

It took a month for Jake and Crystal to figure out who was who.

Jake was quiet most of October. He spend the whole month
reading, so he'd know the history of the place and the struggles of its
immigrants and working people, the poor people from who had come
in waves from England, Scotland, Ireland, Italy and Poland, from Que-
bec, Syria, Portugal, the Azores, Liberia, Nigeria, Columbia and Cape
Verde, and now from Guatemala, Honduras, and El Salvador, all to
work in the mills and to live in cramped overpriced hot-in-summer,
cold-in-winter, lead-poisoned, bed-bug-infested mill housing, people
whose labor had made the mill owners rich.

In late October Jake started to make the rounds. He made
phone calls and met other organizers. He broke bread with the undocumented, the disabled and the poor. He went to meetings at which he
sat in the back and just listened. He went to the State House and sat in
the gallery, learning about how things worked, or, at least, how things
never did seem to quite work out for working people, regardless of who
was right and who was wrong, regardless of what was fair and what was
just and what was smart and what was dumb. He shook hands, went to
the bars where men gathered to tell jokes, and went to libraries and
churches where women gathered so he'd understand their lives as well,
because Jake was someone who always treated everyone equally.

Along the way Jake learned who was who in Providence, Warwick, Cranston, Pawtucket and Central Falls. He learned who ran the
show and how things worked, or if they didn't work, how the people

who ran things got them to run the way they did, so everyone got a little piece, and so nobody who couldn't pay up-front got to rock the boat.

In November Jake hit the street, in full-on organizing mode. The clocks had been turned back so it was dark in the evenings — the sun stayed low on the horizon so there was often sun in your eyes or glare on the windshield when you moved from place to place. Jake transformed himself from a quiet guy at a computer to a man consumed, a man who was on the phone all the time, a man of boundless energy, who was totally, and only, about the work. That was when Crystal and Jake began to encounter one another for the first time and realized how different they were after all.

Jake was from Chicago and though he was young, he had walked the walk. Obama for a little while in 2007, but then Jill Stein once the numbers were nailed down. Occupy in Atlanta and then Portland. Black Lives Matter in St. Louis. Antifa in Charlottesville. A little time at the Industrial Areas Foundation and Asset Based along the way. He knew how to listen, he knew how to shape an issue, and he could work with lawyers when he had to get bills passed and regulations written. He knew how to pull a meeting together, get the media to turn out and sometimes, when the timing was right, he even knew how to get people into the streets. Yes, he was an outside agitator, but no one cared about that shit anymore — Jake lived to make it happen, to make change real, and he lived pedal to the metal, flat out, every single day.

For Jake, organizing was a whole-body experience, a contact sport. You live free when you are totally engaged. No spectators and no prisoners. If you aren't part of the solution, you *are* the problem. We create democracy and liberty in action. Only the dead stand still, and you are going to be dead an awfully long time. It doesn't matter if only five people come out to a meeting or twenty people turn out for a demonstration at the statehouse. It's the keep-on keeping on that matters. People, or sometimes, *the* people, will respond when they are ready, when they are tired of the lies and the bullshit, when they have been objectified enough and can see it for what it is. Frame the issue. Call out the racists and the fascists. Organize, phone bank, and organize again. Chance favors the prepared mind. One day we'll get it right. Venceremos! We will win!

But while Jake organized meetings, painted signs, walked picket lines, made phone calls, spoke at actions and accosted anyone who came within a hundred feet of him, Crystal stayed in the office, doing what she had always done and living how she had always lived.

Crystal had a desk, and that desk was hers. She had a phone that was hers and a computer that was hers and nobody had any business touching either. She didn't approach the people who came into the office. Those people needed to come over to her if they wanted help. She came in at 8:30 when she was feeling up to it and she left at 1:00 pm, more or less. She kept a copy of her job description in her top drawer, and she never did one thing that wasn't in it. She wrote policies, procedures, and memos. Lots of memos. She did what she did. Not one thing more. Not one thing less.

Before long, most of those memos were about Jake. His desk was a mess; he let a volunteer use the copy machine; someone had left the lights on after an evening organizing meeting; Jake had called an ad hoc work group committee together and didn't reserve the conference room before using it.

It didn't take long for Jake to see that Crystal was not a friend, not a colleague and not even a co-worker. She was the enemy incarnate, everything he resisted, all the walls he wanted to tear down. She wasn't like the machine – crony capitalism, the deep state locked in institutional racism, the hegemony of banks and bureaucrats over the lives of working people. She *was* the machine, someone who used her position to stifle the innate creativity of people struggling to be free. Every time Jake started to work on a new issue and every time he identified a group of people who shared a concern, Crystal found a way to deflate his progress. The conference room is booked that day. The Board hasn't approved this strategic direction. It isn't in the budget. Crystal found ways to derail many of the new initiatives Jake began. Pictures of his desk and the storeroom where Jake sometimes slept were circulated to the entire organization. Phone bank lists were lost. Copies of emails were leaked to newspapers and to the organizations that Jake was getting ready to call out publicly. The people Jake brought into the office who were oddly dressed or impolite. They acted in ways that were threatening to women. The workplace had become unsafe. Before long, the Board was discussing the hostile work environment, and was trying to decide which of them – Jake or Crystal – had to go.

One Monday morning, a Pawtucket fireman in most of his gear, wearing boots and fireman's overalls but without his helmet, walked into the office, carrying a room sized air-conditioner on his shoulder. The fireman was forty-five years old and freckled. Fair complexion, ruddy skin. Lots of time outside. Blue eyes, a receding hairline and a big moustache. A big Irish guy, who was used to getting his way. He dropped the air-conditioner on Crystal's desk with a bang. Crystal jumped.

"Got a use for this?" the fireman said.

"It's almost winter," Crystal said. "It's an air-conditioner."

"Give it to an old lady with a bad heart. Kid with asthma, something like that. Out of a warehouse. The warehouse burned but the office was ok. They said clear it out. I saw your sign."

Jake came bounding to the front of the office. He stuck out his hand.

"Great to see you man. Thanks for coming by. I'm Jake."

"Carl, this is Jake," Crystal said. "He organizes the poor people. Carl's a firefighter."

"So you know him?" Jake said.

"Knew him. I live in Pawtucket. I know people."

"Thanks for the AC, man," Jake said.

"No problem," Carl said.

"We're not a warehouse," Crystal said.

"It's all good," Jake said. "We'll find somebody who needs the AC. Hey, we got a meeting tonight about this bill in front of the legislature that..."

"No meetings," Carl said. "I put out fires. I don't start them. Later, Crystal." And then he left, the bells over the door jangling when it closed.

"He works for a really regressive union," Jake said, as soon as Carl was out the door. "Lousy record on diversity. They don't support the fight for fifteen."

"He's a Pawtucket firefighter, for Christ sake," Crystal said. "Not Mahatma Gandhi. Give it a rest, will you? But get this goddamn thing off my desk."

Three days later, there was a little dorm refrigerator sitting in front of the office door when Crystal unlocked it in the morning.

It was Jake and not Crystal who was in the office when Carl came back one night the following week. Three volunteers were on the phones. This time Carl carried a brown paper bag.

"Oxygen sats," he said. "Pulse oximeters. For people who have bad lungs. People drop these off at the station after somebody dies. We got four or five of them. Maybe some of your people can use them. People who can't breathe."

"That's very cool," Jake said. "Very thoughtful. We'll find people who need them. Hey, I gave the air-conditioner away. And we are using the little refrigerator. What got you thinking about us?"

"I don't think about much," Carl said. "I know Crystal."

"She's a critical member of the team," Jake said. "Hey, we have lots of interesting things going on. Sure I can't interest you in coming to a meeting? You part of a union?"

"I don't want no part of any meetings, "Carl said. "I heard Crystal is sick."

"She comes to work every day," Jake said. "She stays in the office. Works for us part time. I'm out in the field."

"So nothing like liver cancer or anything like that. I heard her liver is bad."

"She doesn't talk about herself much," Jake said. "She shows up most days to work. I probably couldn't tell you if I knew more than that, but I don't. There's a pretty cool demonstration at the State House on Saturday. Think anybody in the firehouse might be interested?"

"We don't do demonstrations. We put out fires. Once in a while we have to picket the Mayor over contract stuff. But nobody likes that shit," Carl said.

"So how do you know Crystal?" Jake said.

"That's one long fuckin story. From before you were born. I'll be back," Carl said, and then he was gone, the bells over the door jangling again in his wake.

The war between Jake and Crystal escalated. One day Jake accused Crystal of making racist comments. The next day Crystal accused Jake of submitting false receipts. Each day there was a new insult or accusation, as if they were brother and sister fighting for their mother's or father's attention, or were siblings fighting over their parent's will. Crystal worked in the morning. Jake worked in the afternoon and evening. So they were rarely in the office at the same time, and they kept it that way.

Instead, their war was conducted like any war between two people. It was conducted in silence, by email, and through other people, as each of them said at least something obliquely critical about the other when they spoke to anyone at all who knew or interacted with both. Or as each of them said something much more pointed than that. Before long the war had spread to others, as everyone they knew chose sides, and who would be fired first became the only question still to be answered. But the Board, like some distant, indecipherable God, was itself unable to act. It was also now divided, each person recruited by either Jake or Crystal to take up the cause of one or the other. They were the whole paid staff, just the two of them. So there was no one to mediate a truce, and no one to say that this behavior had to change.

One December early afternoon they found themselves together in the office, despite the better judgment of each. It had been a snowless December, which left the world thin, deprived of leaves and light. The sun, which now rose only ever so barely above the southeast horizon, was already starting to set. It was dark and cold — the magical long red light of summer evenings was only a distant memory. An arctic cold front had enveloped the region in a deep freeze. The city had opened emergency shelters for homeless people who were dying of exposure in the street nonetheless. Pipes froze and burst all over the city. People bundled themselves in long underwear and put on layer upon layer of extra clothing and hurried as they went from car or bus to a home or office, to the extent anyone was willing to be outside at all.

To Jake, the cold was an emergency, which required more of his energy and attention than usual. The city and state needed to be confronted with their failures; the Governor should open the schools and public buildings as sanctuaries to the poor and make sure everyone had food and oil for heat because it was too cold for poor people to go out to shop. To Crystal the cold was a bother: she couldn't go out for her walk at midday, and the office heating system didn't keep the place warm enough. There was no emergency. The city had plenty of plumbers to fix broken pipes. No one Crystal knew was freezing to death: the state opened some emergency shelters to take care of the homeless. No one Crystal knew was going hungry.

Jake had come in early. He was in the office working when Crystal arrived. He was on the telephone, but he raised his hand and pointed at his wrist as if he had a watch, as if to say something about the time-of-day Crystal had chosen to appear.

"What happened to the air-conditioner Carl brought over?" Crystal said.

"I gave that to a family in Elmwood a month ago," Jake said. "Little girl with asthma. They live in a crappy apartment with peeling paint. Absentee landlord. The mother comes to the lead poisoning prevention coalition. They'll have it to use in the summer."

"That was *my* air-conditioner. Carl brought it for *me*," Crystal said.

"That wasn't what Carl said," Jake said. "He said we should find somebody sick who needs it. Which is what I did."

"The hell with what Carl says," Crystal said. "Carl is *my*... contact."

"That's not what we're about," Jake said. "Nothing we do here is for you or for me."

"This is impossible," Crystal said. "You are harassing me."

"I'm not harassing anybody. Or at least I'm trying not to harass anyone. Carl said you go back, that you know him for a long time. He came by one day and brought us more stuff."

"My personal life is none of your damned business," Crystal said. "More harassment."

The bells over the door jangled.

A man with a blue face and a runny nose, lost inside a puffy red down coat and a purple scarf, stumbled through the door. A blast of cold air came with him.

"Close the door, Hector, it's cold," Crystal said.

"Door closed. Door closed," Hector said. He stopped just inside the door. His voice was strained and distant because he was talking from his throat, not his chest. He struggled to say even those few words. He started to cough and wheeze. His eyes were red and wet.

"Come in Hector, "Jake said. 'Do you need a glass of water?"

Hector tried to answer but he was interrupted by a fit of coughing, which kept him from speaking and from catching his breath. He put one hand on a table to steady himself, but he kept coughing, his face strained and ashen. He was a small man with short grey hair and receding hairline, a goatee and tattoos on his neck, and with two blue teardrops tattooed under his left eye.

"Let me help you," Jake said. He came to the door. Hector kept coughing, his body shaking, while Jake grabbed a chair and put it behind him. Hector let himself fall into the chair, still coughing uncontrollably.

Then Crystal was there with a glass of water.

"Take some of this stuff off," she said. She unzipped Hector's coat and unwrapped the long purple scarf from around his neck. But Hector kept coughing.

"What happened?" Jake said.

"Boiler... No heat," Hector whispered as he struggled for air.

"Get me a moist cool cloth," Crystal said. "Now."

Jake, who had been standing by, trotted off.

Crystal helped Hector out of his coat. He was wearing three sweaters underneath it.

"You are going to sweat yourself to death," Crystal said. But Hector still coughed and struggled to speak.

"No air," he whispered, and he leaded over a desk, his head in one hand to steady himself.

"We'll get you air," Crystal said. "Try breathing in through your nose like you are smelling a rose. Nice easy long smooth breaths. Like its spring-time."

For a moment, Hector's cough relented, and he stayed quiet, trying to catch his breath. Jake came back with a wet towel and with a brown paper bag.

Crystal wiped Hector's forehead. She put the towel on the back of his neck.

"Do you have a landlord or do you own the house, I don't remember. There's a program," Jake said.

"Mia madre..." Hector whispered, and then the cough and wheeze started back. He bent over double coughing and his eyes started to bulge out from the force of the cough.

"No questions, how about," Crystal said. "Can't you see he is doing all he can just to breathe. What's in the bag?"

"Carl brought them. He said they're for people who can't breathe. I don't know what you call them and I don't know how they work," Jake said. He handed the bag to Crystal who opened it.

"Pulse oximeters. No shit," Crystal said. She took a small black cube the size of a makeup compact out of the bag, squeezed it open, and stuck it on one of Hector's fingers.

"God only knows the last time anybody checked the batteries," she said. But the little black cube lit up anyway, emitted flashing lights for a few seconds and then it displayed two numbers.

"Goddamn it, your friend Hector here is in trouble," Crystal said. "Call 911."

"I didn't know you had any medical training," Jake said.

"There's a lot you don't know. Let's not have a discussion about strategies and tactics please. Just call 911. Before your buddy Hector here is out on the floor. Because I am pretty fuckin sure you don't know CPR either."

They were two blocks from the fire station. The fire department rolled through the door in under two minutes. A fire engine roared up, sirens screeching and lights flashing, just before rescue got there, but the whole parade, rescue, fire engines and police cards, arrived pretty much at once. They lit up the street with the flashing lights and they blocked traffic.

Carl was on the fire-engine that day, so he showed in fire gear. He walked through the door first and squatted in front of Hector. As soon as EMS arrived, he got out of their way and let his crew do their jobs.

They had Hector boxed and wrapped in about twelve seconds. O_2 on, two liters nasal cannula. Gurney in and Hector on it. Bp 160/94. Pulse 116. Sat 84 percent. Patient diaphoretic and not moving air.

Quick IV in the field, running half normal saline at 125 an hour. Lung-er in exacerbation. Pretty routine. These people, they wreck their lungs smoking and then they fall apart in their fifties. The least challenge does them in – a little infection, a little allergy, even the cold dry air from a big freeze. Their houses are a mess – boilers that don't work, moldy basements, people crowded together like rats. It's a set-up for bad disease. All absentee landlords. The city doesn't do squat to clean these places up.

Boxed and wrapped, and then they were gone. Carl's crew went back to the truck, but Carl lingered. First in, last out. Something like that.

Crystal ignored him at first. She got a broom and began to sweep the floor, sweeping up all the papers and plastic Rescue leaves behind after a call, the wrappers from tubing and the little plastic needle caps and whatnot. The tall Black kid was rearranging the furniture. He pushed the desks and chairs back to where they belonged because the crew had pushed it all out of the way to make room for the gurney. He was clueless, that kid. Lots of energy. And really tall. Reggae man. Rasta man. Something like that.

"You saved the day, lady," Carl said.

"Bullshit," Crystal said, her back towards him. "I just did what I was trained to do. Didn't matter. He would have been out on the floor in another minute or two, and the squad would have scooped him up and run him in just the same."

"He was sick as shit," Carl said.

"They're all sick as shit. Every single one. Each in his or her own way. There's no end to it," Crystal said.

"You too?" Carl said.

"Me too. A little. I'm okay. Nobody lives forever. Listen, Carl, thanks for bringing what you brought, the AC and the sats and so forth. The sat helped today. The kid didn't know what to do. I should have said thank you. I just, you know, I get like this," Crystal said.

"You're welcome. What do they say now? De nada," Carl said.

"And you can bring more... stuff, if it comes to you. Lord knows this whole world is sick. Or poor. Or hurting. Each in their own way. The kid talks to them. They come here. Sometimes we help."

"No sweat. When something comes to me, I'll bring it over," Carl said.

"But nothing about you bringing stuff changes anything between you and me," Crystal said. "That's history. That's over."

"I know that Crystal. I did what I did. You did what you did. We can't get any of it back," Carl said.

"Nobody lives forever," Crystal said. "We can put what you bring by to good use. It's okay to come by when you have something to drop off."

"I will," Carl said. "Nobody lives forever."

The bells over the door jangled as Carl left. There was a blast of bitterly cold air. The heating system blower switched on with a dull roar, countering the cold with a warm wind that seem to come from some other place in time or space.

"So what's the story with you and Carl," Jake said.

"We go back," Crystal said.

Crystal turned, went back to her desk, and woke her computer up so she could finish her work.

Some people will never change, Jake thought. *She's just completely closed off, always secretive, completely unable to say what she thinks or feels. She's probably writing another memo about me.*

But I've got that base covered, he thought. *The moment of reckoning is coming. I've got friends in the community. We're ready. Soon we'll make our move and she'll be gone. We'll shut her down. Fire her ass. Run her out of town. We'll do what we've got to do. Sweep away the old and corrupt. Bring in the new and the just. History is written by the victors. And history will absolve us.*

In his own mind, he envisioned a great battle, in which he and poor and working people everywhere would win a great victory by finally defeating this woman and everything she represented. Jake and those poor and working people would build a new Jerusalem together, which would be everlasting, and racism, selfishness and greed would vanish forever from the earth.

God's Providence

She came from money and was used to getting what she wanted, but all she wanted was to have a good time. She wasn't weird or kinky, nothing like that. For Elizabeth, a good time meant shopping with a girl-friend, walking into a dinner on Ev's arm at the beautiful home of one of their beautiful friends or getting tipsy on Prosecco as they hung around a fire after spending the day on the slopes at Vail or at an outside restaurant on the beach at Nantucket. She loved those friends because they were so much like her that they could almost read her mind. Of all her friends she loved Meredith best, because Meredith had what she had and knew what Elizabeth knew, as if they were sisters from another mother, which was what they sometimes called themselves, even if Meredith lacked Elizabeth's depth and insight and some of the drawing power Elizabeth had in a room. Nothing matters more than knowing you are not alone, than knowing that how you see the world is how the world is, and that was what Meredith did for her: Meredith confirmed that everything Elizabeth believed was true because Meredith believed it too. When Meredith saw what Elizabeth saw and felt what Elizabeth felt, Elizabeth knew what she saw and felt was real.

Elizabeth loved to be the center of attention, and she loved it most when she walked into a room and all eyes turned toward her, the men, all wanting to be with her, consciously or unconsciously, and the women, all a bit jealous, seeing her through the eyes of the men and then all deciding at once to be her friend so their men wouldn't ever dare to think of Elizabeth *that* way, and so they themselves could learn how to do what Elizabeth did, and how to have what Elizabeth had.

Elizabeth was sixty, but you'd never know that unless you were close enough to see the crow's feet around her eyes, or how the skin on her neck had loosened over time. Her eyes still sparkled when she looked at you, which she did without any hesitation, taking in all of you at once, holding nothing in herself back. She was still thin and willowy, almost catlike. The simmering fluidity of her body and her frank speech drove men, particularly tall men, to distraction, or, at least, once had.

These days men still looked, but Elizabeth's intelligence also commanded their respect. Ev, who had left a wife and three children for Elizabeth twenty years ago, was still proud of how she looked and the attention she commanded when she entered a room, even if his interest in what she said and how she said it had flagged somewhat after twelve years of their own marriage. She was childless — her own choice, a choice she had never doubted — but that meant Ev and Elizabeth had little to talk about, other than the passions and dramas of Elizabeth's friends, the deals and connections made by Ev's colleagues and buddies — and getting their calendars to match for social engagements and brief vacations or weekend trips to the beach house or the mountains in the winter.

So Elizabeth wasn't surprised one weekend when Ev couldn't join her in Boston for the symphony. Meredith was in Vail that weekend, so Elizabeth decided to go to Boston alone and spend the weekend walking and thinking. Elizabeth was a little disappointed at first, because she loved walking into Symphony Hall with Ev and attracting the attention of the other concert goers, many of whom Elizabeth knew or knew her. She loved being *that* couple, so elegant, so refined, so well dressed, so confident and so self-assured. But being *that* couple was also kind of a prison, having to live up to so many other people's expectations. Elizabeth could imagine another life, a life where she was free to be who she wanted to be in the moment, free to live only for herself. She began to look forward to that weekend alone, a time when she could slip into the concert free and unencumbered, as if she were a spy looking in on her own life. It had been years since Elizabeth spent any time alone. The thought of it was a breath of fresh air, almost a vacation from what Elizabeth did and had to do every day, the first time in memory that she could make her own choices and be completely invisible.

The weekend itself was even better than Elizabeth imagined it would be. She took Friday afternoon off from work, drove to the city, took a room at the Ritz Carleton, and ate dinner at No. 9 Park, a slow, sumptuous dinner of many tastes and too much excellent wine bought by the glass. She brought Anna Karenina to reread and read it slowly and carefully from a table in the window looking out on Boston Common, savoring each word. In fact, a little snow began to fall, and it dusted the Common with unusual beauty, white snow against the dark night, the lights of the city twinkling in the background, with men and women dressed for winter, bundled in overcoats, hats and scarves, hurrying across the Common, the warmth of their inner lives almost palpable as they walked together, eyes on the ground in front of them so they could maintain their footing, with their purpose – getting from place to place quickly, before they took a chill – clearly defined. Elizabeth let herself get more than a little drunk, and took a cab back to the hotel, even though it was only three blocks away, and she enjoyed that image of herself, staggering out of the cab, immensely.

The next night, Elizabeth wore black pants, a black top, simple pearl earnings, a simple pearl necklace – and no makeup —to the Symphony, to hear Andris Nelsons conduct Bartok, Mozart and Ravel. She snuck into her seat at the last moment, just as the conductor was raising his baton, closed her eyes and let herself dream with the music. Something was changing in her life. She missed Ev, to be sure, but she didn't miss the formalism of their life, the way they did the same thing the same way, year in and year out, doing what worked once over and over as if they were owned by their past. Now Elizabeth felt strangely free. At the same time she recognized with a start that Ev wasn't really present anymore, that neither of them were present, that the life they had built and shaped and that contained them was their life together but neither of them were really alive within that life. Huh, she thought. Fancy that.

Some weeks later, Elizabeth asked Ev about going to New York. Visit Ev's daughter Abby in Brooklyn. Do the show at the Met and see a musical. Too busy now, Ev said, offhandedly. And I don't do musicals, remember. But feel free to take the train down yourself.

I can do that, Elizabeth thought, and wondered for a moment about asking Meredith. But what the hell, she thought, I'm better on my own. She took the train down, met Abby for lunch, breezed through the Met and then took in the musical, all in one day. She stayed over at The Algonquin, slept late and took a mid-afternoon train home. Mission accomplished.

It was not the next week, or the week after that, but three weeks later that Meredith called and asked Elizabeth if she minded if Meredith dropped by for a drink after dinner. Come for dinner, Elizabeth said, and stay for a drink. No Meredith said, I'm tied up for dinner. I'll see you at eight.

Elizabeth was in the kitchen and Ev was reading in the living room when the doorbell rang.

"That's Meredith, dropping by for a drink," Elizabeth said.

"I'll get the door," Ev said. Elizabeth heard the door open before she had time to dry her hands, which was unusual, because Ev rarely even raised his eyes once he had settled into his club chair and began to read.

Then Meredith was in the kitchen. She hugged Elizabeth, held on a little, and lifted the glass of white that Elizabeth poured.

"Come and tell me things," Elizabeth said, knowing the things Meredith had to tell were inconsequential. Then Elizabeth led Meredith into the living room to sit.

Ev was standing near the couch. Meredith went to stand next to him, leaving Elizabeth standing next to Ev's club chair. Elizabeth looked at Meredith and Ev, standing together, and understood everything in that instant.

"Let's do this sitting down," Elizabeth said, and sat of the edge of Ev's chair. Ev and Meredith sat down on the couch together.

"How could you?" Elizabeth said. "But all that doesn't matter now, does it? Let's figure out what comes next and in what order, and see if we can all come out on the other side with a little of our dignity intact, shall we? Not that my dignity mattered much to either of you up until now."

When it was done and she had moved into a beautiful condo overlooking the harbor and downtown, a place with a thousand amenities, Elizabeth took to her bed for a week.

There had been no rancor. Ev paid for everything. Moving was Elizabeth's wish. The house was just a place. The marriage had been a stage, an illusion. Better to start anew, start from the top, and leave the past behind. Still Elizabeth had wounds to nurse. Truth be told, she had looked down on both of them. Ev was good looking and had aged well, but there was no there, there. Elizabeth had been everything in the marriage, the decider and the inspiration. It was her taste that chose and decorated the house, her initiative that made their calendar and took them to events, the theatre and openings, and her friends who made up their social life. There would have been no relationship if not for Elizabeth, and truth be told, no marriage, although in retrospect, perhaps there had never been a relationship or a marriage at all. Even so, losing Ev still smarted, just because Elizabeth had lost something she took to be hers.

But Meredith? Meredith was just Elizabeth's alter-image, the Elizabeth reflection, the woman who had no original ideas of her own. She succeeded by talking like Elizabeth talked, by dressing like Elizabeth dressed, and by going where Elizabeth went. And to think this woman, who Elizabeth trusted, would turn on her like that, could inveigle her way into Elizabeth's home and Elizabeth's life and then, while her back was turned, move into Elizabeth's marriage, empty as it was? Talk about trust betrayed. This woman who Elizabeth didn't really think very much of had just supplanted her. That was what hit Elizabeth hardest. There just wasn't much to Meredith, and somehow, Meredith had come out on top. It made Elizabeth lose her faith in the natural order of things, in any kind of rationality and it made her feel unsafe, as though there was no one she could trust and no one she could love without fear of loss and betrayal.

But after a week in bed in her new home, after a week's bingewatching empty television, Elizabeth dusted herself off, stood herself up and went back to living again with a vengeance.

Or at least that was what she told herself. She started to take long walks, to explore Providence, this small city that she lived outside of but didn't really know. She took up Yoga and got serious about having a weekly massage. She haunted day spas, libraries and bookstores. She attended lectures at the university, had lunch at the Art Club, and made it known that she might consider an appointment to the Council on the Humanities under the right conditions. True, single and married men weren't falling all over her the way they once did, but Elizabeth was a woman of many abilities, and she was in no rush. She'd be ready if and when the right man appeared. If and when. She made no apologies and planned to take no prisoners.

One day in the late spring, Elizabeth took herself to the ocean. She brought a beach chair, a hat and a book. I'll walk out among the piers at Point Judith she thought, to look at the fishing boats and charters, then drive over to East Matunuck, take a long walk on the beach, sit and read for a bit and then go over to the Oyster Bar where the oysters are salty, fresh and sweet, for a glass of wine and something to eat.

I'm ready for an adventure, she thought. A woman alone. Intimidating to some, perhaps. And I'm not twenty-two. Or even forty. But there are fishermen on the boats, runners on the beach, college boys waiting on tables and parking cars and the odd UPS man or plumber or carpenter, driving about for work. Oysters are an aphrodisiac, Elizabeth said to herself, so one must be careful. Elizabeth knew that no oysters were needed to intensify what Elizabeth wanted, however unconscious and self-indulgent her feelings about the day were at that moment. It was time for a small fling.

But there was no one around to take the bait. Even so, it was a glorious day. Elizabeth walked out on the piers. Most of the fishing boats were out at sea. There were a few overweight men in their sixties who were working on the pleasure boats that were tied to the dock, men in torn tee-shirts with thinning hair and potbellies who smoked and swore as they worked, as they sawed, hammered, and drilled. The sun was bright and clean, and its heat had kicked up a gentle breeze from the shore, so the air carried the sweet smells of pollens from all the trees that were in bloom, and that sweet smell mixed with cooking aromas from the clam shacks on the shore, the smell of deep-fried fish and potatoes and stuffed clams, fishy and clean at once. The boats sang as they came against the dock, lifted by wavelets and the lapping water, itself stirred by the wind. And the colors of the day, the red pennants flapping in the wind, the orange life jackets stacked on the dock, the green and blue netting of the lobster traps, and the yellow and white signs of the clam shacks felt alive to Elizabeth as colors had never felt alive before. The hell with Ev and Meredith and all of her life before that moment, she thought. So what if there were no interesting men around. It was good to be alive, glorious to be there, and the hell with all the rest.

Then Elizabeth drove to East Matunuck. Surely there would be men working on restoring the beach, working to build a breakwater and a stone or concrete seawall to protect the thin slip of road and that little peninsula of beach town from the rising seas, the product of the climate change Elizabeth kept reading about and had no reason to doubt because she knew one could never under-estimate the stupidity and greed of the human race. There was hammering and nailing as people worked on their summer cottages and trailers, preparing the village for its summer inhabitants, people from Cranston and Worcester, Framingham, Woonsocket and Pawtucket, the children and grandchildren of mill-workers, who all now worked in banks or in IT but kept coming back to these cramped little cottages every summer. There were pickup trucks parked on the street or driving back and forth on East Matunuck Road, but everyone was focused on their work or in a hurry, and no one noticed Elizabeth.

Still, the beauty of the day was overwhelming. Elizabeth loved the weather-beaten shingles on the houses that lined the street, grey and strong against the sea and the wind, and she loved how the sea made the sand on the beach glisten, and she loved the rocks that stood out in the surf, the waves crashing over them, and she loved the arc of the water thrown up by the waves and the spray about the rocks and she loved the way the sunlight bounced and was refracted by the spray and the mist when a wave hit the rocks. She loved the colors of the rainbow that sunlight produced in the spray and the mist and she loved the churning of water, waves, wind and sun — the stuff of life itself.

The town beach was a few blocks away, so she drove over to it. The beach was empty. She saw a few determined walkers, who were mostly women younger than Elizabeth and who looked like high school teachers, determined women with tan weathered faces wearing windbreakers and carrying small weights on each hand, walking quickly just above the waterline as if they had someplace they had to be in just a few minutes, as if they were counting their steps and needed to get to 10,000 before they hurried off to make dinner or to pick up a child or to stop in at the assisted living facility to check on mom. There was an old couple walking the beach, walking slowly as if lost, as if they had forgotten their purpose in coming to the beach, other than to meander, and there was a mother who was a woman of color in a beach chair, with children who played in the sand while their mother talked on a cell phone. Elizabeth worried for a moment about why the children weren't in school and worried if the mother wasn't in some sort of trouble until she saw a well-dressed man in his late thirties walk up to them quickly and speak to them in Spanish, in a way that suggested that they were tourists, visitors from another country who had come to be together in a place they felt to be exotic, and for a moment Elizabeth was ashamed about her unconscious judgment, and then she was glad to see that all was well, and that this was a family that was happy to be on holiday together.

Elizabeth laid her folded beach chair and book on the ground. She took off her sandals and curled her toes in the warm sand. Then she began to walk near and in the water.

The sand was glorious, silky and warm. It embraced her feet as she walked, welcoming them. The ground shifted a little with each step, so she had to concentrate on walking, to think about maintaining her balance and to throw her hands out to maintain that balance, but even that tiny struggle was good – it let her feel all the muscles of her thighs and her back, and feel the strength she still had, and to take a certain pleasure in the victory of being upright, something she never thought about as she went from place to place or idea to idea or even from passion to passion. The seawater was cool and bright in its way, a shock when it came up and flowed over her feet. The water was far too cold to swim in but still could wash away the lint between her toes, the crusty old skin from her ankles, and any exhaustion Elizabeth still carried from the changes of the winter and spring.

The cold of the water woke Elizabeth and let her feel every nook and cranny of her feet and her toes, the soles and even her calluses. The waves erased her footsteps as she walked so that every step was a step on new soil, on the fresh earth of a new life. The waves compacted the sand and gave Elizabeth a smooth surface to walk on, a surface she loved after the struggle to keep her balance when she walked on the warm but shifting sand. When her feet got too cold, she let herself drift back to the sand, which warmed and embraced her feet again.

She studied the seabirds as she walked, the plovers, scurrying along the sand, darting toward the sea when the waves receded and scurrying out of the way when the waves returned, pausing only long enough to peck at the beach, looking to capture something Elizabeth couldn't see; and the gulls, which drifted on the sea winds, cawing as they flapped and twisted or suddenly dove at the water, fishing, their eyes scanning the surface and into the depths, aware of what Elizabeth didn't know existed – or sometimes coming to rest on the beach, white and specked with brown, their yellow beaks proud and manly, the red crust of flesh at the top of the beak evidence of the power of blood that flows through the veins and arteries of living creatures, evidence that everything alive is connected just by being alive; the gulls sometimes resting, sometimes standing, their bodies pointed into the wind, ready to alight and flap away as soon as Elizabeth came near.

Then the sun started to set, the temperature dropped precipitously, and Elizabeth took herself to the Oyster Bar.

The Oyster Bar sits on a salt pond. They have surrounded their outside deck with plexiglass which shields you from the cold night breeze, and they have gas-fired heaters on the deck that allow you to be inside and outside at once, so you can see the sun setting over the lime green sea grasses, so you can sit outside, surrounded by the real life of the planet, and still be warm.

Elizabeth sat at the bar with a glass of wine, savoring the moment, and ordered dinner. You meet people when you eat dinner at a bar. All kinds of people.

A couple sat at the bar together, watching the TV. They were in their forties, the man trim with neatly cut graying hair, the woman blond with hair that was colorized, neatly made up and wearing a pearl necklace but still appearing relaxed. The man looked like a middle manager of some sort, perhaps at an insurance company — the woman was perhaps a real estate agent or a high school principal.

The Oyster Bar is sophisticated place with valet parking that is crowded in the summer, where you might wait two or three hours for a table in season. People come from Watch Hill and Weekapaug, summer people and weekend visitors, and generally not the people who stay at the little cottages near the beach but even so you never know who you will run into there.

A man sat down. He was old enough to know better but not too old, and well dressed, balding with a shaved head. He wore wire rimmed glasses, a dark tweed jacket and a grey vest. He sat straight and had muscled shoulders. Stocky, as if he'd been in the military, but looked smart, so perhaps he now taught at URI or the Naval War College or even at Brown. Interesting. Possible. Perhaps all was not lost, that day.

The news came on the television. A story about the President, Russia and Syria.

"Make us great again, big boy," the man who was part of the couple said, talking back to the television but so loud that everyone at the bar could hear, his voice deep and tremulous as if he had had a little too much to drink. "Not my president."

"He's everyone's president," the man alone, sitting to Elizabeth's left, responded, talking right over Elizabeth, softly but firmly and loud enough so that the man who was part of the couple could hear him.

"Goddamn traitor. Goddamn Russian spy," the man who was part of the couple said.

"You don't know the half of it," the man alone said.

"Oh yeah? I know what I know," the man who was part of the couple said, too drunk to understand that the man to Elizabeth's left was agreeing with him.

The last thing Elizabeth needed was to be in the middle of a bar fight. The woman wearing pearls, who had been looking away and pretending not to know her partner, now put her hand on that man's shoulder. Elizabeth instinctively put her hand on the other man's forearm, and that man looked at Elizabeth for the first time, in the ancient language of men and women.

"He's out of his mind," she said quietly.

And then Elizabeth felt herself swoon. The room spun, and Elizabeth held onto the man's forearm for balance. She couldn't see light for an instant. How curious, she thought. Just a single glass of wine. Something isn't right. And just as the day was looking up. But she caught herself before she fell over and straightened up.

"Whoo," Elizabeth said. "Perhaps I had one too many myself. Though I'm generally thought of as a woman who can holds her liquor. Not my usual response to a single glass of Chardonnay."

"Not a problem," the man alone said.

And then he ordered dinner.

Elizabeth wondered if the man next to her even noticed her swoon. Got to get that checked out, she thought to herself. Tomorrow.

They talked and then he noticed her more.

They left together. A nightcap at my place.

But in the parking lot, waiting for the valet, Elizabeth swooned again. She reached again for the arm of her new friend, whose name was James.

She heard voices and had a dim memory of flashing lights. And awoke under bright lights, wearing a hospital gown.

The diagnostic vortex. The whirl of thoughts, ideas, threats, presumptive diagnoses based on testing. Retesting. More testing. Second and third opinions. Late night consultations with friends of friends in distant cities. What is it? What does it mean? Why wasn't it recognized before? Can it be treated? What is the treatment like? Risks and benefits. The world's expert in…. US News and World Report's best hospital. NIH and clinical trials. It happened more quickly than could be imagined, and it happened in a way that was agonizingly slow.

First it appeared that Elizabeth had mononucleosis, as strange as that sounds for someone who is sixty. Then it appeared that Elizabeth had porphyria, a poetic sounding name for an obscure disease associated in history with werewolves, with people whose illness made it so they could only come out at night. Then it appeared that Elizabeth had Hepatitis C, a condition that was treatable and had likely been contracted from an old lover because Elizabeth did not and would never have injected drugs, a common cause of hepatitis C, but then love opens you to the choices and foibles of all your lovers and their lovers and their lover's lovers.

Then there was a CT scan and a hurried phone call. Please come by this afternoon — Dr. Strauss wants to talk to you today. Yes today.

And so the drain opened. The waters of the self swirled around as the self disappeared down the drain. Tumors first, in the liver. Then cancer. Of the liver. The liver gone, replaced by tumor. No real hope. People you know and trust, people you know and love who won't look you in the eye. The self shrinking, the picture on the TV shrinking to a dot as the power is turned off. The inescapable truth of a terminal illness, of death arriving on the shuteye flight from LA, of life vanishing in the blink of an eye.

You tell yourself stories as it's happening. This can't be real. They're wrong. They couldn't find the lab test and I had to wait 90 minutes to see the doctor, so clearly they are incompetent – they can't know what they are talking about. I get different stories from everyone I talk to. They keep changing the diagnosis. First they say there is chemotherapy and we'll start next week. Then they talk about radiation, but then they drop that idea. Then they start talking about new drugs that use antibodies. Then they start talking about clinical trials and the NIH.

I just want to crawl into a hole, curl up and die, Elizabeth thought. Do you know what it's like to be stuck in traffic when you feel like crap, when your energy's gone and everything hurts, and you can barely hold your head up? Know what it's like to have to park a car and walk the distance of three football fields just to get in from the parking lot? I don't want to spend every goddamn day in some doctor's office, one doctor after the next, she thought. That isn't living.

It takes a PhD just to remember what they're all called and what they all do: gastroenterologist, hepatologist, hematologist-oncologist, radiation oncologist, surgical oncologist, pharmacologist, pain and palliative care specialist, psychiatrist. Our team. Right. This isn't Sunday and I'm not playing football. They want to make sure that I'm not depressed and that I'm coping. I'm dying at 60. Hello? My husband just dumped me for my best friend. And now my liver has been eaten up by tumors which keep growing while you people argue amongst yourselves about what to do next. Nero fiddles. Rome is in ashes on the ground. They have a whole crowd of social workers and nurses who want to feel my pain – now every emotion even has its own specialist. Could they please wait until I'm dead before they start dissecting me?

James, the guy from the Oyster bar, was nice enough and would have been fine for one night. But he turned out to have a wife from whom he was "estranged" though they lived in the same house. Separate bedrooms, he said. No secrets. All on the up and up, so called. But he faded fast after the first little hospital sent her to Boston, as soon as the so-called experts in Providence started arguing with one another.

It was the third or fourth week, when Elizabeth knew there was trouble but didn't know which kind, before she talked to Ev, who called because he needed her signature on paperwork for the mortgage. She didn't want to tell him. She didn't want to give him the satisfaction. But she backed into it anyway. Hard to get to the lawyer's office for the notary. Kind of busy. Having tests. Blood tests and CT scans and MRIs. They said porphyria and Hepatitis C. But now they think there might be something in the liver. She was waiting for an MRI appointment which hadn't been scheduled yet. One doctor's office needed to talk to another doctor's office. They needed some kind of permission for the health insurance company, who wasn't calling back. Something like that.

And Ev, despite their history and his guilt and his spinelessness, jumped in with both feet. Ev was a pretty connected guy. On boards. The maker of deals. So he knew people who knew people. And the guys at the top, the hospital CEO and the insurance company CEO, they would take his call. Or they would take the call of one of his friends, who all knew how to make people sit up and listen.

So they hopped to, those hospital people. In five minutes, Ev had them scheduling a conference just about Elizabeth, with all the specialists in the same room, and they got the MRI done the same day, no questions asked. How in hell, Elizabeth wondered, do regular people, the people who clean houses and fix boilers and drive pickup trucks, the beauticians and the plumbers and the grocery store clerks of the world cope with getting sick, when they have no Ev and no one to make phone calls to rich friends who can throw their weight around?

And then Meredith was back. She came to Elizabeth's house one night about eight unannounced. She carried a pot of beautiful white calla lilies and a bottle of particularly good Chardonnay, which got awkward when Elizabeth opened the door and Meredith tried to hug Elizabeth to comfort and forgive herself, but the flowers and bottle of wine got in the way. Meredith was crying. Meredith put the flowerpot and the bottle on the floor, and they both laughed because of the clumsiness.

And then they both cried and held on to one another, despite everything.

In Elizabeth's last days, it was Meredith who moved into Elizabeth's house to be with her. Ev came every day, and flitted from place to place, trying to be helpful. But Meredith stayed the night and was there in the depths of the night when Elizabeth awoke from her medicated sleep, dreaming or hallucinating. There was an aide from a home health agency who they hired to be there with them – three aides, actually, because they came in shifts, a woman from Liberia, a woman from Guatemala, and a woman from the Dominican Republic, and these women helped to the extent they could but were mostly silent, like ghosts. They came in and out to bring something to drink, a little something to eat, to answer the door when visitors came, to help reposition Elizabeth in bed and to change the sheets. There was a hospice nurse who came once a day with medications and to check vital signs, although Elizabeth didn't see the purpose of the temperature and blood pressure taking – because it should be plenty obvious when she was dead after she died. But she put up with it all graciously, understanding that these were the ways in which people showed their love, as inadequate as that love was now.

Then quickly, mercifully, Elizabeth fell into a deep sleep, because her liver had failed and all sorts of drugs and toxins accumulated in her blood stream, recalibrating the chemistry of her brain. Her chest moved in and out very slowly, as if whatever small mechanism drives breathing had stopped working, as if Elizabeth herself had left the room and kept forgetting to remember to breathe or to sit up and talk. Her lips pursed when she did draw a breath, as if she were taking air in through a straw or was getting ready to kiss someone, and her skin was moist and unnaturally pale. The hair around her face was wet with sweat, but even so she appeared to be at peace – the skin of her face was relaxed and smooth.

She dreamed. She dreamed first about being sick. About the doctors who had some kind of new drug, some kind of new treatment, just ready to be released. Some doctor Ev had found who is the world's expert and who knows how to treat it. She'll go anywhere, Ev said – Houston, Stanford, Pittsburgh or Seattle or the NIH. But in her dream all Elizabeth wanted was for Ev be quiet, to go away, to stop playing the hero. In her dream she wanted to sit in a chair on a balcony in the warm spring sunshine, see the green leaves, the insects flitting in the sunlight and hear birds chirp and sing.

Then she dreamed about Ev and Meredith. In her dream they were each on a different rudderless boat in a storm, under a cliff, the sky dark and filled with thunderclouds, the wind wild and the sea churning, in a rock-strewn channel, each boat tossed by the huge surf toward the rocky shore. In that dream Elizabeth was on the coast, at the top of a lighthouse that was on a cliff high above the water. The beam of light from the lighthouse would find each of them, from time to time, as they each put on a life vest and dove into the water, hoping to swim to shore. Elizabeth saw herself throw a rope over one shoulder and then dive from the cliff into the cold sea, certain that all three of them would perish. It is so sad to end this way, Elizabeth thought as she flew through the air, diving to her certain death. Still, it had to be done.

But mostly Elizabeth dreamed of her day at the beach. She smelled the stuffed quahogs and fresh fish frying in oil. She saw the colors of the signs, flags and banners, so green, so red, so yellow and so blue, snapping in the wind. She heard the hollow hulls of the boats coming against the mooring, the strange water sounds ascending, like bells of the earth and bells of the deep. And she saw the sun setting over the beach, red and brilliant orange, purple and blue.

Her life was imperfect. She had lived and tried to love but mostly failed. There would be no trace of her. Still, the earth was a good place. Elizabeth loved life itself, and she was so grateful for having lived after all, for the beauty of everything. She had partaken of God's Providence, and it was good, so good.

When her breathing stopped, as the little color there was drained from her cheeks, Ev closed her eyes and kissed her forehead. Meredith hugged her and then Meredith and Ev hugged one another, not certain what to do or what to say to one another since that what had been given to them both had now been taken away.

Nero

When the immigrant caravan crossed the Suchiate River from Ciudad Tecún Umán, Guatemala to Ciudad Hidalgo, Mexico, Raphael Amos ran the numbers in his mind and began to plot his next move. It's all about the numbers, Raphael knew, and any campaign generates predictable numbers with predictable results.

The caravan was made up of Honduran people. Raphael knew Guatemalans and Mexicans. The Guatemalans and Mexicans Raphael knew were decent people, by and large, just like anyone else. Most of the Guatemalans and Mexicans Raphael knew worked hard and didn't complain. Some of the men could be mean drunks. Some of the woman looked like the Madonna, all-suffering but at peace — their lives were hard, most of them worked in factories, or worked nights as office cleaners or worked in McDonald's or Burger King, and many worked two or three jobs to hold body and soul together. Still, you don't really know anything about people from other cultures anyway, about what life means to other people. It is impossible to tell from looking who has a calm and peaceful home life, and whose life is chaos — impossible to tell when a man has another woman or another family on the side or even two other women, and whose daughters run wild or whose sons are drifting off. The women Raphael knew talked quietly among themselves. Some of the young women were hot, but all cultures are like that.

The market segments the population in various ways that are predictable: hard working men buy trucks and chain saws; women watch telenovelas and buy cleaning products; hot women or want-to-be-hot teenagers buy cosmetics, tight designer jeans, lingerie and birth control; and black sheep men buy beer, tequila, vodka, guns, and trucks. That's marketing, not cultural stereotyping. It doesn't matter what culture consumers come from. All that matters is who has a buck and who is willing to spend that buck on what. At the end of the day, all cultures are the same. The proportions may be different. But people are predictable, and their reactions are predictable. The smart money knows how to measure and target market segments, how to predict return on investment, how to keep your head in a crisis, how to find the upside and cover your bets. What does Warren Buffet say? When dark clouds fill the economic skies, they will sometimes rain gold. Rush outdoors carrying washtubs and buckets, not thimbles and teaspoons. Democracy is a fantastic invention. Everyone is equal when it comes to spending money. And no one should ever discriminate on the basis of race, culture, gender, sexual preference or religious preference, especially when it comes to accepting the money consumers want to spend, whenever and however they want to spend it.

The immigrant caravan was a gift from heaven. It was hard for Raphael to believe that the Russians, the Republicans, the Chinese, the Israelis or the Saudis didn't pay off someone who paid off someone else who paid off someone else to get it started. But who started it and how it started didn't matter. Call it a dark money or a dark conspiracy. Call it an act of God. Raphael saw it for what it was. A golden opportunity. Dark skies. Washtubs and buckets.

It's also amazing to consider the opportunities technology has created. You can now build a social media campaign for next to nothing. Email is almost free. That gets you old people. Anybody can make a video, and you can say anything you want about anybody. All you need is something that gets at the deep-seated fears of people, or their private, curious lusts, or even their dull-witted sympathies. Cute puppies. Sob stories. Naked women. Girl-on-girl sex. Instagram. TikToc. Facebook. Seventy-year-old men click on pictures of nineteen-year-old women, the last flare of a setting sun.

The immigrant caravan. You string a campaign together in an afternoon, and if you do it right, do it enough, over and over, then you can sell anything to someone, and you'll make money. Often, lots of money. Evolution has lots of dead ends. All you have to do is find a little pool, a back-eddy in one of the little streams of our culture that contains enough human beings with a smart-phone or computer who can click on a certain idea or image, and then cha-ching! The cash begins to roll in. The world is full of opportunities waiting to be exploited. God is great and glorious and produces bounty for those who know God and walk in God's ways.

The campaign went up on January 23, a Thursday. Twelve million emails, plus Facebook and a little Instagram thrown in for good measure. By morning, 430,000 responses. You hit the right buttons; you get the right responses. Cash in the cash register. Money in the bank. These people have no idea what they were buying or who they were responding to. Nor do they care. They just want to be heard, to have their fears acknowledged, so they don't feel lost in a culture that has abandoned them. So they didn't feel like just a number, in a world that is only numbers, in world that is out of control. People were willing to throw money away. Raphael was willing to catch it. They'd never know – they couldn't know – who Raphael was, where he'd come from or what he believed, to the extent he believed anything.

By January 23, 2020, the day Raphael launched his immigrant caravan campaigns, there were 571 reported cases worldwide of a new Coronavirus that had not yet been named, 267 more cases that had been reported the previous day. 561 of those cases were in China, but cases had also been identified in the US, Thailand, Japan and the Republic of Korea. 16 percent of reported cases were seriously ill, 5 percent critically ill and 4 percent had died. The name of the virus, SARS-CoV-2 (severe acute respiratory syndrome Coronavirus 2) and of the disease Covid-19 (*Coronavirus Disease of 2019*) was announced by the World Health Organization on February 11, 2020. By then, Raphael's campaign had run its course. It worked. He made a little money. There is nothing to fear but fear itself.

But no more immigrant caravans. Everything now was Coronavirus.

He'd put up *those* campaigns when the time was right. There really is a sucker born every minute. Every second. 4.3 suckers born every second, to be exact. You don't believe me? Google it yourself and you'll see.

One day, when Raphael was on the third-floor landing of his mother's house, he heard a thump and some thuds — someone here, moving about.

The third-floor tenant was an anxious Korean woman with two kids. Raphael had come to fix a stuck window. The tenant told him no one was going to be home so it was fine to go in. Raphael had paused to look out the window of the landing. From that window, Raphael could see Route 95, the train tracks, the hospital and the green, pink, yellow

and brown houses on the hill across the '
way and the train-tracks lay. He liked t'
vantage point — for a moment, the ‹
time to wonder about what huma'
land that was supposed to be the la..
streets were supposed to be paved with gold.

He jumped when he heard the noise. It was
think the tenant was home.

Then his mother's cleaning woman came through the door,
rying a vacuum cleaner, a mop, a broom and two yellow plastic pails.
The vacuum cleaner banged against the door frame as the woman came
onto the landing.

"You scared me!" Raphael said.

"You scare yo mas!" the woman said. *You scared me more.*

The cleaning woman was probably Guatemalan. She was
shorter than Raphael but more powerfully built, with long dark hair that
she wore in a ponytail and that hung half-way down her back, strong,
broad shoulders, skin that was smooth and a warm deep brown and was
a different color entirely from Raphael's skin, and she had lustrous deep
brown eyes that were secretive and wise, hidden and knowing.

"English ok?" Raphael said.

"Little bit Anglish," the woman said. "Un pocito."

"You clean here?" Raphael said.

Raphael remembered that the woman was new. She had worked
for them a few months which was better than some. The cleaners who
lasted only a week or two were more trouble than they were worth. His
mother often went through five or six before she found one that stayed
a year or two. And one who actually cleaned, as opposed to one who just
moved things from place to place and left the lights on.

"Si. Aqui," the woman said.

downstairs? My mother's place?"

"
"And other places?"

"Muchos plaices. Aqui. Providance. Juan-stone. Smeethfild. Side. Siempre."

"From Guatemala?" Raphael said.

"Honduras," the woman said.

A new immigrant for sure.

Honduran people were no better or no worse than Raphael's people, he thought. Honduras has gangs and lots of rapes and murders. His people, during the civil wars, had done worse. Honduras has a thug culture now, as far as Raphael could tell. His people were a tribal people, a people of communities, communities that sometimes went to war with each other, communities that each had their own culture, their own language, their own warmth and their own drama, but also their own corruption, violence, and chaos. Then those communities reshuffled into militias and destroyed one another and their country for fourteen years. Now even Raphael's country was all broken up and dirt poor, and those who could leave were scattered all over the globe. Lots of gangs, in Honduras, gangs that got their start in the US. No kind of place for a man who looked like Raphael. Not home. Not in Honduras. And only barely in the US, truth be told.

Honduran. Immigrant caravan. She might know about the next one before it kicked off.

Now *here* was an opportunity. Chance favors the prepared mind.

A different woman came down the steps of the address he had been given in Central Falls, a woman with dark hair and confident eyes in a tight blue satin dress and blue high heels who knew what she was doing with every inch of her body. Surely not Maria the cleaning woman. Someone else.

But it was Maria who got into Raphael's car.

They went to a restaurant on the Hill. It was too cold to sit outside.

"We talk Anglish," Maria said. "To learn."

"Hablo un poco Español," Raphael said.

"Muy bien," Maria said. 'It's good."

"What did you do in Honduras?" Raphael said, and pulled up Google Translate on his cell phone. "Cual trabajo en Honduras?"

"Medico," Maria said. "I am doctor."

"Sí? And you clean houses?"

"Sí. Empezar. To start," Maria said.

"What kind of doctor cleans houses?" Raphael said. You have to talk down to women. Never tell them what you think. Keeps them off balance and coming back for more. Neuro-linguistic psychology. They think you are important. Desired by others. That makes you desired by them. Raphael read all about it in a book.

"Good kind," Maria said, her eyes flashing in a way that said, don't you ever put me down again. *The kind who bends a difficult world to her will*, she thought.

A doctor. Raphael could not believe his luck.

Somewhere out here, a pandemic was brewing, whipping up its own fears and craziness. Dark clouds. And with a doctor, new opportunities.

She wanted something from him. He was sure of it. They all do, and always did. He just had to figure out what. And then perhaps come to an agreement from which both sides benefit.

They went out twice more. Raphael could feel Maria getting closer to him. He teased her with the Audi. With swank places. Al Forno. Entoteca Umberto. One night he took her to Boston, to the Top of the Hub. She teased him back with beautiful clothes, dark eyes with long lashes, and with the smoothness of her skin, which made him forget that she cleaned houses all day and made him think of a woman who lived her life in luxury, for pleasure, on a whim.

And then the world closed. Stay at home. Like an eclipse of the sun. Darkness at the start of the spring. Dread overtaking hope.

But work didn't pause for Raphael.

Suddenly there were hundreds of millions of human beings with nothing to do but look at their cell phones and computers, stumbling about in fear of imminent unpreventable death, people who had nothing to think about except who was to blame for this mess. The President helped stoke the fear, of course. He always helped. China one day. Blue state governors the next. Senile Joe Biden the day after that.

But Raphael knew how to play both sides. And so he stayed busy. He had two lists. Will you stand by and watch us elect a leftist democrat and bring in total socialism? US Billionaires got $434 billion richer during the epidemic! We need to tax them all!

Raphael tried to talk to Maria by phone. That was better than not talking but not by much. The languages. They stumbled over words. It was hard to listen. Your soul stays inside when you are thinking, when you are searching for a word you don't know or barely remember, when you are trying to sort out masculine and feminine endings or tenses. Their heat had come from being together, from seeing and feeling each other struggle to connect, from reading each other's faces and gestures.

And from the teasing, the flaunting of worlds, hopes, desires, and expectations. That just didn't happen by phone.

Maria had to stop cleaning. No one wanted a cleaner from Central Falls in their house now. Raphael wrote and sent the checks every week anyway. It was the decent thing to do. Maria had three kids. This shutdown wasn't going to last forever. Chance favors the prepared mind *and* the aware wallet.

The end of winter became the beginning of spring. The forsythia bloomed; brilliant yellow gold entwined in a spindly tan bramble. Birds returned. Daffodils and tulips appeared and then disappeared – yellow again, and then red or pink or purple or blue, first a cup of color, then petals of color on the ground at the feet of green stems and broad dark green leaves. There was light in the morning and at night. The air filled with pollens, a pale yellow-white dust that sweetened the spring coastal breezes. Still, the world felt strange. Raphael climbed to the third-floor landing from time to time to look out over the highway and railroad tracks and to see the houses and mustard-colored brick buildings on the next hill.

Now there was no traffic on Route 95. Few trucks. Raphael missed the grunt and rumble of the sixteen-wheelers all day and all night, chugging through the rain and the darkness. Life felt empty, the way a man who has lost a leg perceives its absence, and checks, over and over again to see if the leg is really gone.

Early one evening in late April, Mama called Raphael. She never called to chat. She called when she wanted something.

"Ta bo Maria cleanup gi," Mama said. "She si." *Please take a box over to Maria the cleaning woman. She's sick.*

Raphael hadn't said anything to Mama about Maria. And he didn't think Maria had said anything to his mother either. His mother was just doing her thing, ignoring people most of the time, and then marching in to take over their lives whenever it suited her.

Ain't nobody's business but my own, Raphael thought.

"Le bo a do," Mama said. "Si pep dar. Do ga insi." *Leave the box at the door. Don't go inside. There are sick people there.*

"Yeah Mama," Raphael said. "Yo se." *Anything you say.*

Raphael put on a mask and gloves. He'd never been inside Maria's house. They said Central Falls was infected, that everyone was sick, but it didn't look different — the same old rickety wooden triple-deckers crammed together like boxes and jars in a packed refrigerator. No lawns or yards. No trees. Cars lining the streets and parked everywhere there wasn't a building.

It was evening. The sun was low on the horizon. The light was warm and strong, although the air had cooled.

Maria came to the door in a nightgown and a mask and stood behind the storm door. She looked like she had been run over by a truck. Her eyes were red and glazed over. Her once beautiful dark brown hair was matted and wet with sweat, and her skin, which had been smooth and lustrous, was now pitted and hollow. She looked like a sponge that had been rung out and curled as it dried.

Raphael put the box on a table that stood next to a rusting porch slider. Then he went away.

That night he started to read online. There is no cure for this Coronavirus. There was nothing he could do for Maria. Everyone in that house would get sick. Most likely everyone would recover. Some might die. Maria was a doctor. She knew what to do. Raphael didn't.

There is a little gadget, something called a pulse oximeter, that lets you know if you are in danger. A link in the post about pulse oximeters took him to a website. You can order them on-line. $38.99. Raphael ordered one for Maria. Amazon Prime. He even paid extra for next day delivery. $38.99 for the gadget, $14.98 next day shipping and somehow, miraculously, no tax. $53.97. Not terrible.

And then it hit him. If he was buying a pulse oximeter for Maria, a couple of hundred thousand or a couple of million people were also ordering one for someone they knew or for themselves. Everyone was terrified. There was now something to fear. Dark Skies. Washtubs and wheelbarrows, not thimbles.

What was the most outrageous way to frame that fear? *Exclusive Secret Gadget Used By Both CIA and Russian Intelligence Saves the Lives of the Rich and Famous.*

The campaign formed itself in Raphael's mind.

It's all about the numbers, Raphael knew. Every campaign generates predictable numbers with predictable results.

Snow

They were getting creamed in New York and DC but it wasn't snowing in Rhode Island yet. Jack Holland hunched over a cup of black Dunkin' Donuts coffee and watched the auditorium fill up around him. Another wasted Saturday.

The early arrivals were mostly Asian medical students who clustered around the coffee table in the back, talking to each other. The organizers and speakers stood at the podium in front, loading PowerPoints and making sure the remote for the projector worked. The mayor wanted Holland to come, so he came, but it wasn't clear what he was going to get out of being there. The doctors were all there to learn how to prescribe Bup aka suboxone, the drug of the month, the new silver bullet that was supposed to stamp out drug addiction. Right. Like Bup wasn't already available on the street. These bright young doctors were going to get rich running Bup clinics, a hundred bucks a patient, twenty patients a day, five days a week. That's what, ten thousand bucks a week, and half a mill a year. While they pretended they were so much better than the dealers on the street.

But not Jack Holland. Jack Holland was an EMT. He was never going to get rich, not on Bup, not on nothing else. He ran Rescue in Washington City, the poorest city in the state. His squad specialized in drunks, psychotics and ODs. Drug overdoses were the new hot thing in health care because now everyone was dying of them; the rich and the poor, the urban and the rural, the suburbs and the city — people were dying like flies all over now. Washington City was the capital city of ODs, one or two a week, forever ad infinitem. Man down. Run over hot. The bodies slumped over on the toilet, the works on the sink, sometimes the needle still in the vein. Or just laid out in Jackson Park under one of the big copper beach trees like they were taking a nap. If the body was still warm, they'd start CPR and run 'em to the ER. If the body was cold, they'd just call the medical examiner and wait until someone came to take the stiff to the morgue. ODs had been Holland's life for the last twenty-three years, for as long as he'd been on the squad, and he knew the drill.

But new mayor, new priorities. Hard to predict how much the world changes. Washington City had been all Irish and Canuck with a little bit of Polish, a little bit of Syrian and the first couple of Colombians when Holland was growing up. He himself was half and half – Irish and Canuck, despite the name, but he was third generation American already. It was his great-grandparents who came here to work in the mills. They all died young, before Holland was born, so he didn't even remember anyone with an accent. Maybe his family had been Irish and Canuck once but his people were one hundred percent American now. Yeah, make America great again. That's real. All the rest is bullshit.

The new people were all Spanish. Seventy percent of Washington City was now Spanish. More if you counted the illegals, who you can't ever count because you are not supposed to know they are here. The mayor was Guatemalan. Most of the City Council was Latino. The stores on Main Street were now all bodegas, Central American restaurants or Spanish barbers and hairdressers. The goddamn pizza place was run by Salvadorans. The old people in the high rises were still Irish and Canuck, but they were the poor Irish and Canuck who had been left behind, the millworkers who lived their whole lives in triple-deckers and now had no other place to go after their kids moved to the suburbs or to Texas or Arizona for jobs in real estate, logistics or computer software.

The police and the fire department and rescue, they were still mostly Irish. Now those boys all lived in the suburbs. The union was pretty good, but the union knew, and Holland knew, that the days of the Irish working for the city were numbered. The new recruits were Spanish and African-American. Some — too many — were women. Even so those new kids trained up pretty good, and they came out looking just like the Irish kids looked, wiry and strong, the men with crew cuts and the women with their hair pulled back behind their heads. They all had the same kind of *can't surprise me or wear me down* attitude. They all knew that people who were sick were going to die anyway. Most of their calls now were from people are just trying to get over, just calling rescue to build a good story, so the ER docs would give them Percs or Oxys to sell. It didn't matter that the new kids were a different color or that they could actually speak to the people they picked up. Everybody still knew the score.

Addiction is a Disease. Recovery is Possible. Treatment is Available. The first slide was up on the screen. The auditorium was three quarters full now. People were settling into their seats. A woman came into Holland's row and settled herself one chair over. She was a large woman, dark skinned, with neat dreadlocks. She also had a cup of Dunkin' Donuts coffee. She folded her coat into the seat between them and put her hands around her coffee cup to warm them.

"Snowing yet?" Holland said. "They are calling for four to six."

"Six to ten where I live," the woman said. "Along the coast." She had an accent, something a little British, maybe Caribbean. Barbados or Jamaican, something like that.

"You work in South County?" Holland said.

"No, in Washington Park, in the health center," the woman said.

"Hey, I work in Washington Park. Rescue. I'm your EMS director. Jack Holland," he said, and put out his hand.

"Joanna Briggs," the woman said. She shook Holland's hand. Her hand was soft and moist but she had a good grip, for a woman.

"I'm one of the doctors in the health center. You're here for a suboxone permit?"

"Naw," Holland said. "I'm here because the mayor and my chief made me come. EMTs don't prescribe. Drug overdose is the disease of the month. The politicians think the sky is falling because somebody put a picture of a syringe and a baby on the front page of the newspaper. I'm supposed to learn what you people are doing with suboxone and to network, right? You and me, we live like this. We see that some people live and some people die. You do dope, you die. That's the way it was thirty years ago. That's the way it is today and that's how it's going to be tomorrow, next week, and next year, until the next disease of the month comes along."

The lights dimmed. The speakers began speaking.

First the politicians spoke, naming one another so everyone in the room would know which of them was there. They each congratulated one another for each other's great leadership, reading the talking points about human suffering and hope that their communications people had prepared for them.

Then the Department of Health and the CDC came on with charts and graphs, talking about how the sky is falling. Then the experts spoke, taking all day to say what they could have said in fifteen minutes, using language they thought only they knew about a problem that, if you listened closely to them, they thought only they could fix. Holland was warmer now and unzipped his jacket. He got ready to drift off.

Joanna Briggs, Holland thought. Dr. Briggs. Dr. Joanna Briggs. Dr. Briggs. Couldn't be. That was twenty years ago. Common name. Holland had never met that Dr. Briggs. He always thought Dr. Briggs was a guy. English. And white.

"Where are you from, Dr. Briggs?" Holland said when they were between speakers.

"I'm from Rhode Island," Dr. Briggs said. "I was born in Nassau, in the Bahamas, and that is where my accent is from, but my parents came here when I was small. I grew up in Pawtucket. Yourself?"

"From Washington City. Half Canuck, half Irish. Here all my life," Holland said.

The speakers began again.

They got their start at Lupo's when it was still on Westminster. In those days there were a bunch of them, white guys, Irish and French Canadian, a Polack or two, and sometimes an Italian from Johnston or Cranston, who hung together. They moved around at night, between Lupo's, the Met, that Irish bar on Dexter in Pawtucket across the street from the skating rink and the Ocean Mist in Matunuck. And all the bars in between. They were cops and firemen, EMTs and cable guys, a plumber and an electrician or two. Lots of the cops and firemen did house painting or contracting on the side and came after they were done in the summer, hot and sweaty and needing a beer.

Mostly they came for the music and stayed for the beer. Or maybe they came for the beer and the music was there anyway. Or maybe they came to hang out and there was music and beer and on a good night, women. Lots of women came and went, all trying to worm their way into the scene, but none of them ever completely succeeded. It was after Desert Storm but before 9/11, and a bunch of the guys were in the Guard, mostly as MPs from a unit out of Quonset, and those guys got called up for Kuwait but were in and out so quick there wasn't time for them to be missed. The guys in the MP unit came back with good stories to tell even though no one got shot up bad or hurt, so the stories were stories without pain. Not like what happened to the guys in Afghanistan or good old Iraqi Freedom. By and large the Rhode Island guys lucked out then too. Not always though.

Maureen was a foxy little thing from Fairlawn, Jimmy Moses's sister, blue-eyed with straw colored hair that she wore pulled back into two little ponytails that hung to her shoulders. She chewed gum, even when she was dancing, and she liked tight jeans and tank tops that let you see her boobs which were plentiful and also a decent run of cleavage, so your imagination didn't have to work too hard when she came into the room. She was smarter than most – she was an x-ray tech at Rhode Island Hospital, and she made good money – better than most of the guys – so she could have done better for herself, a doctor or a lawyer or an accountant, maybe, which was just to say she didn't have to run with them but she ran with them anyway and was always dancing when there was music, always ready for a good time. She bounced from one guy to the next and she always danced with different guys, even when it looked like she was with one guy for a couple of weeks. Holland wasn't sure but he had the idea that she never went home alone.

But Holland wasn't a dancer. He'd sit at a table with his hurt leg up on a chair or he'd hang out on the bar, watching, and he figured she was only interested in guys who danced. The guys drank some but not usually too much. Some nights more. They were cops and EMTs and firemen, so they always kept an eye out for each other. Friends don't let friends, hell, you know the drill.

But one night at Lupo's before the music started, when Holland was sitting at a table and a couple of the guys who had just come in were still at the bar getting drinks, Maureen came over and put her hand on his shoulder and then on his arm. She sat down next to him.

"I don't dance," Holland said.

"I can teach you," Maureen said.

"I've seen you work the room," Holland said.

"I don't work the room," Maureen said. "I like people. I like that everyone is a little different, and I like to learn what makes each person tick. So what makes you tick?"

"I don't tick. I tock," Holland said.

The lights dimmed and the band started, loud, funky and electric. Holland couldn't see or hear Maureen for a couple of seconds, and Holland didn't know what the hell to think. And then he noticed his brain was racing, and that he wasn't thinking at all but there was a shit-eating grin on his face.

"Stand up," Maureen said, as soon as the band was between songs. "And don't you dare dance. I'm going to dance for both of us."

So Holland stood with a beer in one hand while Maureen danced in from of him, and eventually he began to sway and move his head. She made him smile, that Maureen, in spite of himself. She was just a kid. Jimmy Moses's sister.

Then there was a slow dance. She had a tight little body, that Maureen, and it felt too damn good to have her pressed up against him as he stood there, as she moved for both of them.

There was a fifteen-minute coffee break.

Dr. Briggs was looking at her iPhone. It didn't make any sense. All that stuff with Maureen was a long time ago. Most of the guys had moved away. Some had already retired. Nobody remembered that old stuff.

Then, Dr. Briggs looked up, and she started to scan the room as if to see whether anyone she knew was there.

"So you ever spent any time at Rhode Island Hospital?" Holland said.

"Not for a long time," Dr. Briggs said. "A little time when I was a resident. Family Medicine. We did pediatrics and some electives there. That was twenty years ago. They treated us poorly. I guess they treated everyone poorly. I'm on the staff of Memorial now. But I never go there either. We don't take care of our own patients in the hospital now. Hospitalists do that. I go to the hospital for meetings now but only once in a while. You work there?'

"Naw," Holland said. "I spent a little time there when I was doing an EMT course back when I was just a fireman. In the Emergency Department. Learning to take blood pressures and start IVs. Now I'm in the ED every day. At Memorial and at Miriam. Sometimes Rhode Island. I know all the nurses and the techs at Rhode Island. I knew somebody…"

The speaker at the front tapped her finger on the ball of the microphone, and a loud BUMP BUMP BUMP echoed in the room.

'Let's get started," the speaker said.

The room went dark. A new slide was projected on the screen over the head of the speaker. Bright yellow font on a navy background, with pictures of kids scattered around the text.

Holland looked out a window. The sky was so grey it was almost green. Holland could feel the snow coming, but nothing was falling. They were calling for four to six. Nothing yet though.

And then they were a thing. Jack Holland and Maureen.

It was a wild time but it was a good time. A couple of weeks. It would be a good time for a couple of weeks. Nothing gambled nothing

lost. She never stuck with any one guy for long
to be dumped, and was always jumpy wh⌐
home. *I can ride with the punches, I'm tough ⌐*
it's worth it, Holland thought. What do they cau
tached? Stupid to get your emotions wrapped up in son⌐
Enjoy it while it lasts. It was pretty good. Maybe even really ⌐

That was back before cell phones. So you called. And m⌐,
you got the voice mail, but then you didn't know if the person was out
or if maybe they were there and screening their calls unless they picked
up. And maybe you drove by their house if they didn't pick up to see if
their car was there, and just to see if there was any other car you knew
in the driveway or parked across the street. What do they call it in the
emergency management world? Situational awareness.

But she was really into him, that Maureen. Didn't make any
sense. She could have had any guy she wanted, cop or fireman or doctor
or lawyer. Anyone, and it was really cool that she wanted him, Jack Holland, although it never quite made sense. Maybe she liked it that he
didn't talk much, so she could do all the talking and he'd just sit there,
looking at her, taking her in, enjoying her and every second and only
half listening. He liked to look at those smart eyes because she was so
much smarter than Jack would ever be, and he liked to think about that
hot little body, and he liked to rest one hand on her thigh under the
table when they sat together drinking, just holding that warm flesh, as if
it would be there for him forever, there to keep him juiced up. Maybe
she liked his hurt leg. She would stroke it when then were in bed together, and handle the hard knob where the bones had come together,
and where you could feel the steel screws deep in his flesh, as if she was
reaching for a place she'd never be able to touch, as if she wanted to hold
what was hot and cold at once and feel a feeling she'd never felt before.

They drank. A lot. Too much, looking back. But they were
_, they could hold their liquor and it let them be loose and free.

Two weeks turned into two months. Jack never thought it
ould last. He had never been into a woman like he was into Maureen.
Two months turned into six months. Six months turned into a year. She
was wild and free, that Maureen. Always doing crazy things. Thinking
crazy things. Wanting crazy things. And Jack, he was totally into her,
even as he waited, expecting to be dumped, and then every day he
wasn't dumped was kind of a celebration, a completely different life, a
life he could never have imagined and certainly never could have imagined for himself.

One late afternoon in March of 1999 Jack called her and got her
voice on the answering machine. It was after she was done with work, at
the end of the day but while there was still light, though the light was
thin and pale-yellow. He was coming off an overnight shift. He was supposed to go home and sleep until eleven, and then they were going to
meet up at a piano bar downtown, over at Davol Square, which was
classier than the kind of place they usually hit.

But Jack couldn't sleep. He called her again. Maureen still
wasn't picking up. If she wasn't home where the hell was she? Jack
thought. Yeah, it was just a matter of time, but he wasn't done, not yet.
Maybe he could find her before she hooked up with someone else.
Maybe he could head her off at the pass. Who the hell did she think she
was, getting to him like this and then moving on?

He got into his car. You don't always think straight when you
didn't sleep the night before. He'd find her. There were only a couple of
places she could be. He'd find her and have it out with her. Truth is truth.
He could take it. They were adults. No need for anybody to be sneaking
around.

Her car wasn't in front of her house but he rang the bell and banged on the door anyway. He drove to the Green Bar but she wasn't there either. A bunch of guys were there so he had a beer, as much from habit as from thirst, and then an Irish whiskey and waited to see if she'd show and who she'd come in with. Then he headed to the East Avenue and parked in the back. He sunk down into his seat and just sat in his car, waiting for a few minutes, but no one he knew came in or out.

She wasn't inside. He had another beer and sat at the bar, looking at his watch. Tommy Cairns came in with Jill Puleo, and they were joined by a couple of guys from the Providence squad, so he had another beer with them, and then Jill said something about going out to the car to do a couple of lines but Jack wasn't ready to be zoned like that. He was awake and on edge and just settling into a mean drunk so he had a Scotch and waited until Tommy and Jill came back from the parking lot. Then he had another Scotch. Then he shoved off.

He drove over to Blackstone Boulevard and then down to Pitman and over to Gano and then to Wickenden. The Coffee Exchange was closed and dark. There were college kids walking on the street near the Indian restaurant and the pizza place but no sign of Maureen.

The piano bar was empty. The piano was there, in the center of the room, but no one was playing. Jack sat in a booth and drank. It sucked to be losing Maureen. What was he thinking in the first place? He knew from the beginning they'd end up like this. It was nine-thirty. Then ten. Then ten-thirty. Jack was sitting so he could see the door but he wasn't looking at the door or anyplace else. He was working hard not to think about her or himself or them and he wasn't looking at the door at all, except when he was.

Then there she was.

Maureen bounced in all business wearing a skirt and a sweater and her straw-colored hair swept to one side, looking fresh like she had just stepped out of the shower. Chewing gum. Damn her.

When Jack didn't stand, Maureen leaned over and kissed the top of his head.

"I brought you a present," she said, and put a small, wrinkled brown paper bag on the table. "Man, we're going to have fun tonight. You ready for something different?"

"Where the hell were you?" Jack said.

"What do you mean?" Maureen said. "It's eleven o'clock. Like on the dime. We were supposed to meet here at eleven. What's with you?"

"I mean where were you before? I called you. You weren't at your house and you weren't anywhere else."

"You came over to my house? Didn't you just get up?"

"I couldn't sleep. I drove by your house. No Maureen. You weren't at the Green Bar or the East Avenue. No Maureen any of them places. Where the hell were you?"

"Out. You know what? Fuck you. I brought you a present. You can go fuck yourself. I'm going to the Ladies Room."

Maureen stood, her jaw clenched and her eyes squinty, like she was bound and determined not to give an inch and not to cry. She swept the wrinkled brown paper bag off the table.

"I don't need you for this," she said, and Jack took her to mean only that she didn't need him to give her shit about just trying to live her life.

I'm being stupid, Jack thought as soon as she was gone. *It's all in my head.* He ordered another drink. *I'll fix it when she comes back.*

But she didn't come back.

I'm a fool, Jack thought. He got a strange empty feeling in his stomach. *I better go fix it. Apologize and all that shit. I'll drive over to her house. I got to own this one. This one is all on me.*

But her car was still in the parking lot.

Where the hell is she, Jack thought. *In the Ladies' Room all this time? What the hell is going on?*

So he went back in the piano bar, more confused than drunk and more drunk than pissed off at himself for fucking this one up.

Then somebody was yelling for help. That yell came from deep in the bowels of the place, near the kitchen. Jack ran hot, full steam towards the yell, which turned out to be coming from the Ladies' Room.

Maureen was in a stall, slumped over and blue. There was a set of works on the blue tile floor next to her. A waitress and a cook were in the stall, holding Maureen up, yelling for help, but they had no fucking idea what they were doing. Or what they were dealing with.

He knew she was dead as soon as he touched her. When he lifted her, she was light and heavy at the same time – easier to lift than most of the bodies he had lifted, but dead weight, and so not Maureen. Her body was still warm, but not hot like Maureen's body was. He carried her out of the stall, lowered her to the ground, and started CPR. He heard the sirens and then he heard them get closer. But they just weren't close enough. Not then. Not ever. Would never be close enough, ever again.

Providence showed and pushed him out of the way. First they took over CPR. Then they stuck on AED pads like there was something left to save. There was a rhythm so all they did was bag her.

Maureen got a little color back but she stayed waxy and white, her skin cool to the touch. He prayed that they weren't too late.

But he knew. In the back of his mind he knew how much time had elapsed. Twenty, maybe thirty minutes before he got out of his seat to go find her. Another five or ten in the parking lot. Brains need oxygen. Jack was no rocket scientist, but he could add. And subtract. And multiply. And divide.

They rushed her into the truck, but Jack knew the game was over. He drove his own car right on their tail as they ran hot.

It was just a couple of blocks. They got her tubed in the ED and sent her straight to the ICU.

He stayed three days straight until they ran the EEG. He knew. No brain activity. Nothing left. Her skin was white and her flesh, her face, her arms and her legs got bloated. Then he couldn't stand to look at her anymore.

So he called every day. She was twenty-seven, goddamn it, and you don't just turn off the ventilator on a twenty-seven-year-old who was so full of life. Her parents and Jimmy stood guard. She was theirs again.

He called every day and he talked to the resident in the unit that month.

Dr. Briggs.

They broke for lunch. Dr. Briggs went back to looking at her phone. Then she stood without looking at Holland and walked to the back of the room to get her boxed lunch.

The snow had started to fall, big broad flakes that dropped to the ground with determination. A thick fog of falling flakes. A blanket hanging in the air, too dense to see through. Holland imagined that the people outside were hurrying to get home, hurrying to the store to get their batteries, milk, and bread and then go home and hunker down for the storm. He imagined that people had turned up their collars and were covering their heads because the snow was thick and moist, the kind of snow that coats your hair and falls into your eyes, that works its way under your collar and sends a chill right through you, into your core.

Wish I had the four-wheel drive, Holland thought. *Looks like the weatherman was right this time. At least four to six. Six to ten on the coast.*

Dr. Briggs was in the back, talking.

That other Dr. Briggs, the one for Maureen, the guy Holland knew only as a voice on the phone was a white guy. Holland was sure of it. He listened to the voice again in his mind, the voice he hadn't thought about or heard in twenty years. He wasn't so helpful, that Dr. Briggs, although there was nothing he could do. He didn't seem to remember Jack from call to call. He didn't get what Jack was going through. Her condition hasn't changed. Her vital signs are stable, at first. That was all he would say, that Dr. Briggs. Like Jack was some distant cousin, calling for a weather report. And then, she's hemodynamically stable, after Holland told Dr. Briggs he was an EMT. No spontaneous movement. No evidence of brain activity. There's always hope, but we are being realistic and talking to the family about options. Then, chronic vegetative state. That Dr. Briggs was always in a hurry, his voice clipped and precise. Common name. Probably just a coincidence.

The speaker tapped on the end of the microphone with her hand.

"Would everyone get lunch and return to your seats? This is an eight-hour course, and we have to do eight hours for you to get credit. But because of the snow we want to get started again as soon as we can, so we can get you out of here before the roads get worse. Five minutes."

Holland got up. There were only a few boxed lunches left. Turkey-on-rye or vegetarian.

Dr. Briggs caught his eye again as they were sitting down.

"Snowing at a pretty good pace now," Holland said. "I hope they do get us out early. Even though it's Saturday. 95 is going to be a bear."

"I don't know the people on Rescue in Washington City," Dr. Briggs said. "Your guys help us out two or three times a week. Perhaps we can collaborate a little more."

"Good idea. Hey Doctor. So you didn't work in the ICU at Rhode Island in the late nineties? I had a friend there."

The lights dimmed, the projector came on, and the speakers began to drone on again. The PA system was louder than it needed to be. There was feedback which made the speaker shrink back from the microphone for a moment until the amplification was adjusted.

Dr. Briggs looked like she was going to answer but stopped and turned her head to the front so she could see the slides.

A year later, it was Dr. Briggs who told Holland the plan. Maureen had been on the vent for a year. Dr. Briggs came back to the ICU every few months, and he would take Jack's calls when he was there. Jack called in every day but he couldn't stand to go there. His hands would shake before each phone call. This was him. His. He had done this. For a year, Jack spoke mostly to nurses. Then they took Maureen out of the ICU and she spent ten or eleven months on a vent unit in Jane Brown, waiting for a bed at Eleanor Slater.

Then one day she was back in the ICU when Jack called, and it was Dr. Briggs on the telephone again.

"Do you want to be here?" Dr. Briggs said.

"I call in," Jack said.

"Her brother said everyone wanted to be with her. The plan is for extubation at about eight thirty tomorrow, right after morning rounds. There's a surgical team standing by. Hard decision," Briggs said.

"What decision?" Holland said.

"Extubation. Organ harvest. Very hard. Very sad. The right choice."

For a moment, Holland felt like they had extubated *him*. No air. Room spinning. Can't tell up from down.

"You're the fiancé, right? Okay for you to be here. Probably better, psychologically. Closure. Tough case."

He went then. Right then. Just after dark.

It was only barely Maureen. He recognized her by the way her hair was parted in the middle and tied on both sides of her head. That reminded him of the ponytails and the way she chewed gun while she danced. Her face was white and waxen, almost a little blue, like ice. The respirator whooshed in and slowly out, lifting Maureen's chest for her with each incoming breath, her chest and lips rising and falling like the incoming tide, the sound of expiration like the water draining out among the rocks at the shore, so clear and final that Jack pictured the rocks and the shells at the beach tumbling over one another as the tide receded and he heard the water rushing and crackling through the rocks.

Only barely Maureen. There was peace in the room, a great holy peace. He stood with her for an hour, and held her hand, which was cool and flaccid, as if she had already withdrawn from her body. He watched her chest rise and fall.

And then he felt her presence, like she was next to him, talking. Or standing in front of him, chewing gum while she danced. Only lighter than that. He had the sense that she wanted him there, that she had been missing him and wanted to talk to him, to be with him. And now here he was.

Maureen was peaceful. The sun was setting. The room filled with light.

She didn't talk, of course. She didn't move or blink. But he heard her anyway. *Have a life,* she said. *Find someone who loves you. I didn't mean to hurt myself that night. I only wanted us to be together more intensely.*

Jack stroked her cheek and leaned over and kissed her forehead, and he felt his chest start to shake, so he backed out, stifled his shaking and he blocked a goddamned tear. He stuffed all that he was feeling back into his chest, and he walked out of the ICU cubicle where she lay dying while he was still a man, before he lost that too.

He checked at the ICU desk. Dr. Briggs was gone for the night.

The talk ended. The last slide was of the speaker's three children waving on a beach surrounded by palm trees. There was polite applause.

The lights came on.

A moderator came to the microphone.

"We're going to cut this short," the moderator said. "It's snowing hard now. It's two forty-five. If everyone goes on-line and reviews the last slide set and completes the post-test, that will give you your required eight hours. Then you need to apply to the FDA for a waiver and set up your own offices to do suboxone. We have assembled a list of mentors to help get you started. We hope you will all begin prescribing and help us get the thousands of people dependent or addicted to opiates on medication-assisted therapy. Good luck, and thanks for coming out on such a lousy day."

People began to stand. There was the bustle of voices, the smack and clacking of desks and chair seats being closed, the rustling of clothing and the stamping of feet.

"My ex-husband worked at Rhode Island about twenty years ago," Dr. Briggs said. "He was an internist who trained in pulmonary critical care. He rarely left the ICU. Maybe he knew your friend."

"My fiancée," Holland said. "She died in the ICU after a prolonged hospital stay."

"I'm sorry," Dr. Briggs said. "I'm sorry for your loss. I hope they took good care of her and took good care of you. My ex-husband is a very smart man. He is very good at what he does. But sometimes he can be a little brusque. Sometimes it is hard for him to listen."

"It was okay," Holland said. "Everyone was okay. It was a long time ago. Seems like in another world. Hey, hope to work together a little bit. Lots of ground to cover. I figure we're better if we all talk to each other."

"I'm looking forward to it," Dr. Briggs said, and she held out a gloved hand. "Stay warm and dry. There's nothing we can't do if we do it together."

The snow was falling in big slow flakes that coated Holland's hair and eyebrows and fell inside his collar. There were already six inches on the ground so after a few footsteps there was snow in his shoes. Holland could only see a few inches in front of him. The city was white and quiet. Cars were moving very slowly through the streets, which had not yet been plowed.

I should have brought the goddamned four-wheel drive, Holland thought. *It's going to take me hours to get home.*

Addiction is a disease. Treatment is available. Recovery is possible.

Maybe.

Maybe not.

The Death Spiral

As Jack Shandy-McCoy stood crowd duty at the Senator's community dinner, he concluded that humankind had reached the end of its rope, that this was the end of the world as we know it. These weren't poor people. They weren't angry Black people, chanting that garbage about Black Lives Matter. These were rich people, doctors and lawyers and professors, all dressed up like it was the sixties, in jeans and down coats. The men wore bandannas, watch caps and baseball hats, and some of the women wore those stupid pink pussy hats, while others wore fine woolen coats, with brilliant yellow and green silk scarves, and beneath the scarves Jack was sure those women wore pearls.

It wasn't a huge crowd but it was big enough to be ugly and it felt as ugly as any crowd Jack had ever managed, uglier than the crowds at Lupo's, the Met, the Dunk or at Brown Stadium. These people felt more rowdy, more restive than the drunken punks who hang around Lupo's and the Met. This group was packed into the vestibule of a junior high school. They banged on the doors and chanted slogans that didn't make any sense. Jack stood like a statue in uniform in front of the locked door, his hands behind his back, taller and bigger than most of the men, a symbol of something – what, of order, of civic might, of propriety, or even of command and control – a symbol of something that matters, something Jack couldn't quite name. A symbol, but at the same time

Jack understood that he was completely invisible as a person. People in crowd saw a statue when then saw him, a likeness of a cop but not a living human being. At times like this you become the uniform and the uniform becomes you. It's useful cover. You can see without being seen, even though you are there, and can hear without ever speaking.

But though the crowd was rowdy and though Jack was there by himself, he felt no fear. The unit commander, five or six motorcycle cops and even a deputy chief were on scene on the other side of the locked glass doors, standing with the Senator's people, shepherding people with tickets in and out of the community dinner and being a show of force inside the auditorium, which was packed full of people who themselves were pretty rowdy.

Jack felt no fear because he wasn't a guy who did fear. He was big, he was in uniform, and though he wasn't completely in control, he had a whole force behind him, and though these people were acting up, Jack knew he could handle them, that they would respect his authority should he choose to exert himself. He was invisible to them now, but he knew exactly how to make himself seen when he wanted to be seen and respected when he wanted to be respected.

The crowd was milling about, talking about strategy and tactics and how fucking angry they were about executive orders and cabinet appointments and about what the President did yesterday.

A young woman in her twenties or thirties who was wearing hiking boots and a down coat and no makeup tried to catch Jack's eye and say something lame, thanking him for his service and so forth. But Jack wanted to stay invisible, so he pretended he didn't see or hear her. You got to keep your focus. The rest of them acted like he was a servant, a guard dog, who they could order to heel according to their ugly, arrogant mood.

When a young guy with a double teardrop and whose neck and arms were covered in green and blue tattoos squirmed his way into the vestibule, Jack made him in a second and threw his shoulders back. He took a deep breath, making himself bigger, the human version of a puff adder, or a stallion that stands at attention when a dog comes into the field where his harem of mares is grazing, raising his head, pointing his ears, flaring his nostrils, and inflating his chest to make himself bigger and broader, so the intruder knows who is in charge, and knows not to come any closer. The dude with the teardrop snaked through the crowd, hunched over, head down. He wore a worn olive-cloth Army Surplus greatcoat that made him look more street. The kid had red eyes that made him look like he needed a fix and a runny nose that he kept whipping on the back on his hand. Jack was doubted that anyone else in the crowd gave the kid a second thought. The kid slipped between the densely packed knots of people, finding little pockets where no one was standing and slipping between those pockets, inserting himself into the spaces that were more theoretical than real but finding those spaces and moving through them nonetheless.

That asshole wasn't anybody from the East Side. That asshole was trouble.

The asshole made Jack about the same time Jack made him, and angled himself away from Jack, edging to Jack's right as he wormed his way through the crowd, headed to the glass doors at the front. Quick list of scenarios. The kid was just a punk, here to pick the pockets of the rich. Possible, but who comes to a goddamn demonstration to pick pockets? The kid was a mass murderer and there was a sawn-off shotgun inside the cloth coat. Also possible, but quite a stretch. There's no need to get yourself to the front of a crowd if you are a shooter. You can kill hundreds perfectly well by shooting them in the back. The kid looked like a homeboy junkie who had done time, not Al Qaida, but you can never tell. And just up to no good.

Not the time to be a statue though. Jack looped his thumbs over his belt so his hand was near his service revolver and he pushed through the crowd so that he would be where the asshole was headed before the asshole arrived, but he did it slowly, so he could stay invisible. No plan. Just cop instinct, Wayne Gretsky style. Don't be where the puck is. Be where the puck is going. Punk, in this instance. Still, the back of Jack's mind was screaming, back-up, back-up. This was a plenty peaceful crowd, however rowdy. But just let a cop apprehend an offender in front of five hundred do-gooders, just let Jack figure out that the pest had a knife or a gun and was up to trouble and then push him against the wall to disarm him, and all those fuckin' liberals would go bat-shit. In a crowd like this, anything could happen. And was probably about to, now that this little punk was in the mix.

They met in front of a locked glass door. Through the door you could see the auditorium, filled, even overflowing with people.

Just then some idiot grabbed a doorhandle near Jack and started to shake the door while the crowd started to chant, "Come outside, Come outside," and "This is what democracy looks like," all loud enough so as to drown out any speaking that might be happening on the other side of those glass doors. If this is what democracy looks like, Jack thought, sign me up for something else. They have no idea how good they have it, Jack thought. Somebody needs to be in charge, and make America great again, because this sure ain't even close to good. This is a fucking mess. How the hell am I going to do my job and keep these god-damn people safe?

Jack put his body between the punk and the doors, ready for anything. There ain't going to be no monkey business on my watch, Jack thought.

But the kid didn't back down or slink away like Jack expected. He stood up straighter himself. What do you know? There was something familiar about this kid.

"Hey Officer Shandy-McCoy. Good to see you, man. These people are nuts. How are your kids?"

"Who wants to know?" Jack said.

"I'm Billy Santucci. Larry Santucci's kid. I came up with Lucy. St. Rocco's and then LaSalle."

"Billy Santucci. You look different, brother. How's your mom?" Jack said.

"Hanging in there. We all went through some changes after my dad died. But I've got my shit together now."

"Good to hear, Billy. Good to hear. I'm sorry for your loss and your trouble. What are *you* doing *here*?" Jack said, and he stepped it down a couple of notches, thinking, this is somebody I know. Billy's father had been a cop in Pawtucket. Solid guy. Caught cancer and died a couple of years back. Kid got into drugs and dealing and ended up in the ACI. Sad story. Billy Santucci might be messed up now but he's one of us. He's my people. Which makes him safe.

We're good, Jack thought.

Jack exhaled, and let his chest shrink a little.

"This is all out of control," Billy said. "These people are crazy. Somebody needs to stand up. I came to tell the Senator to get with the program, to speak for all of us, for the regular people of America and not just the rich and famous."

"I think you're outnumbered, Billy. The people inside are all just talking to themselves. Big echo chamber. Circular firing squad. Goddamn big circle jerk. But it doesn't matter. The hall is filled. I can't let you or anybody else in now. They say the Senator is coming out here in about a half hour, and that he'll take questions then."

"I got to get into that hall, Officer Shandy-McCoy. I got to stop this craziness. You ever hear Whitehouse talk? He don't come from Rhode Island. He don't know squat about me or you or the people we are or the lives we lead. All that bullshit about climate change and Obamacare. He's the banks, man. He's the oil companies and the cell phone companies and the goddamn EPA. That dude *is* the swamp."

All of a sudden, the voice in the back of Jack's brain started squawking. There was a crazy look in Billy Santucci's eyes. *Backup*, the voice in Jack's brain started to say again. *Backup*. Maybe we are not so good after all.

Jack hit the trouble button on the squawk-box with one hand, unsnapped his night-stick with the other and leaned in so his body was between Billy and the glass doors. Billy, backing away from Jack's bulk, found himself pushed toward the green cinderblock wall on the side of the vestibule.

"I got to get into that hall," Billy said.

"You get your shit together right *now*," Jack said. He said it low and deep so as not to disturb the crowd, but the people milling next to him noticed anyway. They saw Billy and they saw Jack for the first time when they saw Jack stand up. When they heard his voice. The people next to Billy and Jack turned their heads to watch and at the same time took a half step away, getting ready to run.

"Fuck you," Billy said. "I'm going in."

"You'll go where I tell you to go and do what I tell you to do," Jack said.

Jack didn't see the weapon, but he knew it was there. He turned and used his shoulder to slam Billy against the wall. Then he grabbed both of Billy's arms and bend them behind Billy's back so the kid could only stand straight, the kid's upper arms nearly popping out of his shoulder joints and Jack in complete control of the Billy's torso. The gun clattered on the cold marble floor. Jack cuffed Billy's hands behind his back as a flying wedge of three motorcycle cops wearing blue helmets burst through the glass doors while Jack was cuffing Billy, and they stood point around Jack.

The people in the vestibule shrank back and then surged forward, both frightened and drawn to what was happening. They saw something but they weren't sure what it meant, and they were flummoxed between their need to run for cover, their morbid curiosity, and their endless irrational outrage.

The four cops all knew that their mission was to get the gun off the floor and get this offender back through the glass doors before more trouble started. They didn't have much time.

"Hey," some guy in the crowd shouted.

One of the blue helmeted cops flipped on a rubber glove, grabbed the gun and put it into a plastic bag.

"God damn it," somebody else in the crowd yelled. The crowd began to push forward as a uniform from inside the glass doors opened the doors. Jack pushed Billy toward the open door, but suddenly there were three young women in the way, their arms locked around one another's waists.

"We will not be moved!" the shortest of the three women shouted, and then everyone in the whole goddamn vestibule started singing a goddamn protest song, so loud that Jack couldn't hear himself think. The last thing Jack Shandy-McCoy needed right then was a goddamn protest movement or sit-down strike. This was Providence Rhode Island in 2017, not Selma Alabama in 1965 and all these goddamn people were rich white people, not poor Black people who had been shat on for four hundred years. There was a wise guy with a gun who was ready to shoot someone if Jack hadn't stopped him. Couldn't these goddamn people tell the difference?

That was when the woman in the down coat and hiking shoes piped up.

"Mic check!" she yelled.

"Mic check!" five or six people close to her yelled back.

"Mic check!" the ten or fifteen people closest to the first five yelled, and then everyone close-by in the vestibule started snapping their fingers.

Then the crowd started to quiet as its attention shifted to the woman in the down coat and hiking boots.

Jack had no idea what the hell had just happened or why and he didn't care one bit. The second that the three women whose arms were locked around one another's waists turned to look at the woman in the down coat, Jack shoved Billy through the glass doors and the three motorcycle cops followed just a step behind them. They slammed the glass doors shut and locked the doors again. Then Jack pushed Billy out a side door to a cruiser waiting to take him downtown to be booked, with the motorcycle cop who had picked up the gun trailing half a step behind, on his way to forensics.

It's a miracle humankind has survived this long, Jack thought, as he turned his cruiser around on Summit to climb the hill on the way to the office. We are pretty fucked up. People on one side wild and crazy like Billy. People on the other side like lemmings, all looking and acting alike, and never questioning their assumptions. Each heaping insult onto injury. We're getting to the point that we have nothing civil to say to one another, like we are two separate nations with nothing in common, on track to have a civil war, like the country is in a death spiral, plummeting through the clouds and unable to see where we are or who we are and not having any idea that the ground is rushing up to meet us.

But then you don't know where salvation is going to come from. That young woman, Jack thought, she knew exactly what she was doing. I stopped this punk, sure, but she saved my ass. She paid attention, kept her wits about her, and pulled that rabbit out of a hat at exactly the right moment as if she and I were talking together, working together, and were of one mind.

Maybe we *can* do this after all, Jack thought. Maybe, if enough people can think like humans and act like people when the chips are down, maybe we'll survive this stupidity, this time when no one is thinking or listening, but only talking, only chanting slogans so loud that nobody can hear themselves think.

Billy was hunched in the back seat, cuffed to the car door. Poor kid, Jack thought. Poor stupid, stupid kid, suckered by one temptation or one hallucination after the next, and then sucker punched when his dad died. Judge is never going to let him out of the ACI. Repeat offender? It's going to be years. You don't show up at an event like that with a loaded gun. And you sure as hell don't do that on the East Side. The kid's going to be in jail for fuckin ever, until his craziness burns itself out or he dies of old age. Which for a kid who had spent too much time on the streets is probably fifty. Live by the sword, die by the sword. The gunslinger's creed. Or something like that.

"I'm on Boxes. Gonna need my meds," Billy said, as Jack unhooked him from the back of the unit and stood him up. "And a doctor. You goddamn brutalized me in that place. I think you broke my goddamn shoulders."

"March," Jack said. "We're gonna get you booked. You know the drill. Booked. Holding cell overnight. Then over to Intake in the morning with the rest of the overnight crew. You can see the doctor there."

"They don't have no goddamn doctors at Intake. At least not right away. All they got is nurses for the first couple of hours and I'll be sick by then."

"Maybe you should have thought of that before you pulled your little stunt," Jack said, and almost added, you little weasel, but he thought the better of it and kept his mouth shut. You don't profit by rubbing it in, Jack thought. The kid is likely down for the rest of his life.

Little weasel, though, was exactly what Billy was. The kid was a little weasel, a little varmint, darting from place to place, looking for a little carrion here, a slow mouse or chipmunk there, or for half a sandwich somebody had thrown away and put out in the trash. A little weasel with no self-control.

But at the same time, this is Larry Santucci's kid. Came up with Lucy. He could have been Jack's kid just as easily, Jack's own son. You just don't know how it's all going to turn out.

They came through security and into the dimly lit hallway that leads to the holding cells. There was an officer at the desk. Jack would turn over custody, and then spend two fuckin'-some hours writing the whole thing up.

"Mic check, "Billy yelled.

"Knock it off," Jack said. "There's nobody to fall for that bullshit here."

We are always just an inch away from disaster, Jack thought. The differences between us are meaningless. The death spiral is always sucking at our feet. Those same words had saved Jack's ass maybe thirty minutes ago. Here those words were bullshit, just the whining of a little junkie, hungry for a fix. Though you are supposed to say person with substance use disorder now. Junkie communicates stigma, and stigma is bad in this crazy new world, where up is down, down is up and you never get to say what you really think.

That woman saved my ass, Jack said. Maybe down is up, Jack thought. Maybe I'm wrong, and we will all start saving each other's ass, and maybe we really are on a highway to the sky.

"Thank you for not totally busting my ass," Billy said, as one of the inside guys took custody and started to lead him away. "My old man was right. You are a stand-up guy."

Jack got into the elevator and turned around in time to see the inside guy leading Billy away. Then the elevator doors closed, right in front of his face.

The Deer Stand of the Dead Deer Hunter

(A story with two endings)

What Collins don't know won't hurt him, Rosa Bah thought as she climbed the ladder that lifted her into that tree. You shouldn't have a ladder there if there ain't no one to climb it. All that man thinks about is work. Got to take a break sometimes and look around.

Truth be, there was nothing but trees to look at from the little stand at the top. Rosa was up in the branches so most of what she saw was leaves and branches and more trees. She could see into the right-of-way, into a clearing between the stone walls, a little paddock someone must have used for goats years ago. Rosa didn't know that this was sheep country, not goat country, that goats had never caught on much in the good old USA, and that goats and donkeys were part only of the country she had left behind. She had never seen a deer, so she couldn't imagine a 16-point buck bedded down between those walls or grazing quietly when it thought no one could see it. I am the queen of all I can see, she thought, though I can't see very much. Who puts a ladder into trees?

If Rosa had a cigarette, she would have smoked it, right then and there, dropped the butt, coated with her purple lipstick, and watched it fall end over end into the brown leaves below, just to mark the place.

But she had no smokes so no butts and no purple lipstick, and the place stayed Collins' place for the present. At least she had done something Collins told her *not* to do, which was to climb that ladder.

She was halfway back to the barn when she saw Collins, old, white and barrel-chested, his back stiff and his gait a little unsteady, dressed in those worn old barn boots and overalls from another century, almost from another planet, breathing hard as he walked up the wooded hill.

"Get lost?" Collins said.

"Got your berries picked. Fifty quarts. Plenty berries," Rosa said. Behind her, in a trailer behind the ATV she was riding, sat 50 quarts of raspberries, almost twice what she had been sent to pick and all the berries that were ripe that day.

"Go over to the strawberries next to the barn," Collins said. "Grace is there. She'll tell you what to do."

There was always what to do. Grace was Mrs. Collins. She was as quiet and flinty as her husband, but she dressed better, a tired old white woman with skin drawn tight over her cheekbones and a wrinkled neck, who wore her almost white hair behind her head in a bun, and who always wore tiny pearl earrings even when she was working on the farm. Mrs. Collins ran the store and the market garden. Her husband did the field crops, the corn maze and the hay, and between them they were always working. Strange that two old white people still had to work. Their people had been here long enough. You'd think they'd just sell out, let the farm become tract houses and move to Florida or Arizona, which is where all old white people go to die.

It was a crazy crazy idea when you stopped to think about it. Send immigrant kids from the city out to the few remaining farms to learn farm-to-table. Rosa's people made a garden at home, but no one ever thought anything of it. That was just for them to eat: cassava greens, plantains, and pineapple. The women planted and hoed. The men took down trees and made trouble. Here they try to make it seem like food is art or more important than family: they take pictures of their food, and you can go to school for it, just like you go to school for a teacher or a doctor or a lawyer or a priest. There were classes taught by white people with beards and kerchiefs that she had to sit still for before Rosa was sent to this farm, way out beyond Greenville. Maybe there was another kind of class she could have taken after she got her GED. But the Youth-Rise people were totally focused on this thing, that Rosa would be a farmer, building on the strengths of her culture and so forth, so her neighbor people would have healthy food and the vegetables they liked to eat. Rosa didn't care anything for farming or about the pictures of food. Those men in beards and the women wearing kerchiefs talked about farming like they were in church and farming was God himself. But she didn't have much else to do and this sounded way better than working at McDonald's or Dunkin' Donuts.

Sounded better but probably wasn't better. She worked all the time on this farm. She picked raspberries, hoed rows of strawberry plants, weeded the melon patch, unloaded bags of chicken feed, cleaned out the chicken coops, set up irrigation systems, or waited on customers in the store.

Rosa had just finished picking the end of the day strawberries from the pick-your-own patch before it was time for her to go, and then Grace said, "Go find Walter please, I need him in the store while I'm getting dinner." So Rosa walked up the hill, back towards the raspberry patch. But Collins wasn't on the road and he wasn't in the raspberry patch and he wasn't in the woods past the raspberry patch where they had a shed for the chainsaws that Collins used to take down trees for cordwood and to cut logs for the little mushroom operation that he had going under some old oak trees. He wasn't working the beehives that lined an open field on the side of the hill.

Rosa was back in the woods when she heard a man's voice, and there was Collins, up in that tree with the ladder in it, talking to himself, and moving his hands this way and that.

"Mr. Collins," Rosa said, but Collins went on talking.

"Mr. Collins," she said again, louder this time.

Collins paused, as if he thought he heard something, but he went on talking.

By now Rosa was standing right under the tree, thinking about how she was going to get Collins down. The ladder shook as Collins called out, and the leaves of the nearby branches whooshed as Collins batted them out of his way as he moved his arms. There isn't room for two on a deer stand. It's just a ladder with a place to stand at the top and a bar you can hold or rest a gun on.

"Charlie in that tree," Collins said, as if he was calling out to someone who wasn't there. "Charlie behind the wall. Get down, get down, get down! Incoming, incoming, incoming!"

"Mr. Collins!" Rosa said, and then she reached a little. "Walter!" There was no way in hell she was going up that ladder to bring Collins down. He was going to have to come down alone.

"He's not coming home, Grace," Collins said.

"Dinner time, Walter," Rosa said. "Come down from that tree," she said in Mrs. Collins' voice.

Collins stopped gesticulating. The ladder went still for a moment, and then it shook as he came down, one heavy boot after the next. Crazy-crazy, these old white people.

Rosa held out her arm as they walked back on the rocky woods road and Collins held on to it to stabilize himself. He was able to walk, but he wasn't entirely back to himself. Then he went into the house

without closing the barn door and
you tomorrow at eight sharp,' whic
day before she left.

So Rosa closed the barn do(

Collins was back to himself .
stern. The day started clear but the a
came up. "You go work the strawberr
worked them, glad that the sun wasn'   .., yει. Even so
there wasn't any shade in the strawberry field. It was hot work.

Then they let her work the store for a few hours. Easy time. People come to pick-your-own. You give them buckets. Then tell them the
rules (No sandals or high heels. Wear sunscreen and a hat. Drink plenty
of fluids. No climbing on the tractors or farm implements. Pack out your
trash.) Weigh and box what they've picked and then ring them out.
Only a few people ever noticed that pick-your-own was twice the price
of already picked, and those few people just shrug and laugh at themselves, realizing they had just paid good money for the privilege of doing
extra work. Crazy-crazy country. Crazy-crazy people.

Rosa took her lunch at the counter. Then Mrs. Collins came to
mind the store. She sent Rosa to pick raspberries again, but first made
sure Rosa had a big floppy hat to wear and a long- sleeved shirt to cover
her arms. She sent a lunch for Mr. Collins with Rosa.

Collins was working with a chainsaw in the woods near the deer
stand, working in orange chainsaw chaps with a bright orange helmet,
ear protectors and a screen that covered his face. His back was turned
so he didn't see Rosa when she drove up on the ATV. He was limbing a
shagbark hickory he had dropped the year before, that lay hinged above
the forest floor twenty or thirty yards from the deer stand. He worked

tree toward the base. The branches of the hickory ...d as they left the trunk – no branch was straight – but ...had a certain majesty in its asymmetry. The chainsaw ...and smoked, revving for each cut and quieted to simple quiet ...s between cuts. With each cut a shower of wood chips spewed out of the screaming saw-engine and the smoke became most intense.

Collins cut one twisted limb, let it drop and then stepped over it to cut the next. There was a rhythm to his work – the saw whined, spit out smoke and woodchips, a limb crashed to the forest floor, then Collins stepped over that limb, lowered the saw onto the next limb, and then the saw whined and smoke and wood chips sprayed out again. Collins didn't look left or right or up or down. He just worked, at peace, as if there was no other life and no other world.

Collins worked one side of the tree and then shut the saw down so he could pile the cut branches off to the side between two trees. Shafts of light filtered through the trees to the forest floor. The moment the chainsaw stopped, Rosa could hear the scutter and chirping of the birds and squirrels again.

Rosa waved but Collins didn't see her.

"Mr. Collins," she said, louder. He didn't turn. His ears were covered by hearing protectors.

So Rosa tapped on his shoulder.

Collins jumped. When he turned, his eyes were out of focus, and he looked extra old like he did when he came down the ladder.

Rosa held out his lunch pail.

"Don't you ever come up on a man working with a chainsaw," he said. "This is dangerous business."

Rosa waited. She spent most of her life waiting and she was good at it.

"Thank you for bringing my lunch," Collins said. "We have work to do."

"What do you see up that ladder?" Rosa said.

"You don't touch that deer stand neither," Collins said. "Every tool has a purpose, and if you don't use it right someone can get hurt."

"What's the purpose of the deer stand?" Rosa said.

"Hunting. Hunting deer," Collins said.

"Do you hunt?" Rosa said.

"Nope," Collins said. "Not anymore. But it's not my deer stand."

"Whose deer stand is it?" Rosa said.

"No one you know," Collins said. "Grace send you up for raspberries?"

"I do raspberries. I'm not afraid to work," Rosa said.

"My son's deer stand," Collins said. "He put it up and then got himself killed."

"Sorry for that," Rosa said.

"No more hunting for me, no hunting ever again," Collins said. He took the lunch pail, stood it under the deer stand itself, put his helmet and ear protectors back on and pulled the start rope of the chainsaw, which screamed back to life.

An hour after Rosa started the raspberries, the sky clouded over and a wind came up. Then the sky got dark. Rosa heard thunder in the distance, and the wind became strong. Rosa thought she had time to finish so she kept picking, but then darkness enveloped her, the wind stopped, and the birds stopped chirping.

A hard splash of rain fell and then stopped. We're gonna get wet, Rosa thought, so she started moving the boxes of berries under the cart behind the ATV, hoping to keep them dry.

Suddenly, boom! Everything was white. The earth rocked. Rosa was pitched forward. Wind and gushers of water beat on her head, face, ears, neck and back. The air was black. The ground and trees shook and shook and shook again.

The top of a tree on the edge of the berry field crashed to the ground. Rosa ran under the biggest tree. The wind became fierce. Rain slapped down in sheets. It soaked Rosa's hair and clothing. Water streamed over her eyes, neck, belly, legs, and back.

The white birches on the edge of the field bent horizontal, bowing at the waist. The cart behind the ATV flipped on its side and tilted the four-wheeler so one set of wheels lifted off the ground; one grip of the handlebar got stuck in the mud while the other waved in the air.

Then the storm passed.

Rosa wiped the water from her eyes and pulled her hair off her forehead. The soggy, pale green cardboard berry boxes were scattered everywhere, the raspberries themselves were just dull red humps and pockmarks on the brown forest floor.

She heard a voice in the woods.

The woods were littered with downed trees, some broken in half.

Collins lay under a tree in the mud. The tree he was cutting had come down on his legs. He was working to free one leg from his boot, and calling out for his wife, one call every few minutes. The other leg was bent below the knee at a strange angle. His skin was waxy and white, and his teeth were chattering.

"I'll get help," Rosa said.

"No time for help," Collins said. "Cut me loose."

Rosa, who had no problem picking berries, driving the ATV or even climbing the deer stand, had no idea what Collins meant. Cutting Collins loose meant cutting the tree on his legs with the chainsaw, which was lying on its side in the mud, a few feet away. She had never even touched a chainsaw and didn't intend to start now.

"I'll get help," Rosa said. This man needed the fire department to come with equipment and EMTs. Rosa needed to be out of there.

First ending:

"You leave me here and I'm gonna die," Collins said. "I'm bleeding to death inside my goddamn boot. My leg is broke. I can feel the bone of it poking through the skin and my foot feels like it's sitting in water. I bet that's blood not water and this trembling is what happens when a person goes into shock. There's no help that's coming up this road soon. We had a good burst and trees are down everywhere. If you don't cut me loose now that help will only get to reclaim the body, and that body would be mine."

"I'll call for help," Rosa said. Her cell phone was wet but it was still on. One bar.

"Call away," Collins said. "Then pick up that chainsaw and I'll talk you through cutting me loose."

The chainsaw was a heavy orange box with a handle, some knobs, levers, a trigger, and a toothed bar that stuck out savagely from one side, like an anxious virgin's nightmare about the male organ. Collins was right. 911 took her information and said they'd dispatch right away but it might take an hour or more, there were trees down all over.

Collins got weaker. He was as white as a man's white shirt and wasn't breathing right now, pausing between words or phrases.

"Flip the little lever that says 'stop'", he said, and paused, "as you pull on the trigger." Pause. "There under the handle." Pause. "No, under that handle." Pause. "The trigger."

None of this made sense to Rosa, but she followed the man's instructions. She flipped different levers and knobs as he said yes and no and waved his hands or pointed.

"No choke. The engine's still hot," Collins said. His voice was weak and trailed off at the end of each sentence. "You've got it." Pause. "Now put the saw on the ground." Pause. "And pull the start cord."

The engine caught on the third pull. It put-putted, thumping like the tail of a dog that was still but wanted to go out. Smoke and hot exhaust came from underneath the engine.

Rosa needed both hands and her back to lift the saw. She dropped it on the log a few feet away from Collins' leg. The saw was too big for her, awkward and unbalanced. There was no way she could run it, no way she could cut. The engine wanted to fall to one side, and it took most of her strength just to hold the bar straight.

Then she pulled the trigger. The saw jumped and cried out. It jerked forward. It spit and it smoked and it screamed. Rosa held on but then she was frightened by the noise and smoke and pure violence of the saw, so she let go of the trigger.

Everything stopped. The saw quieted. She could hear sirens in the distance.

There was a cut in the wood. She'd made a cut. It was a few inches deep. She could cut wood after all. She could work a chainsaw. She could cut Collins free.

She looked at Collins but he was quiet and looked paler yet. The Rescue would have to cut through downed trees to get a truck up the woods road to where she and Collins were. She squeezed the trigger again.

Rosa made a cut a few feet from one side of Collins's leg, and then a second cut a few feet from the other side. The log on Collins's leg shifted. Collins stirred only enough to groan. Then he fell back into what looked like sleep.

Rosa lifted the free section of log and rolled it out of the way. Collins was free. She rolled Collins over.

"I ain't dead yet," Collins said.

"You will be soon if we don't get you out of here," Rosa said.

"I'll carry you out on my shoulders," Collins said.

"I don't think so," Rosa said. "I might be able to help you up but I can't lift you. You can't walk on that leg." She looked around, took a few steps, found a forked branch on the forest floor and leaned it against the trunk of the fallen tree. Then she stomped it with one foot so it broke where she wanted it to break. She handed it to Collins.

"Put this under your arm on the side of the bad leg," she said. "Throw your other arm around me. Maybe you walk some that way."

Collins grunted. He grabbed onto Rosa's arm and let her pull him to sitting, then to a half stand on his one good leg, and then he stood up to his full height. He put one arm around Rosa and without thinking tried to put his bad leg on the ground. He groaned with the pain, his face got whiter still, sweat poured from his brow and he almost fell over, but Rosa leaned under him, took the bulk of his weight on her back, and shoved the forked branch under the arm on the side of his bad leg. He steadied and then got his balance back.

They started to hobble down the hill together. Collins was almost twice Rosa's size but she held him up anyway, and they made slow progress down the hill. Whatever else happens, Rosa thought, I'm not going to let this old man fall.

Four firemen with a backboard met them as they came through the trees. Collins lay across Rosa's shoulders, his good foot on the ground, his bad foot dragging. He was limp. He was able to put weight on the good foot each time Rosa paused.

It took all four men to carry him the rest of the way on the backboard. They huffed and puffed. They worked on him for ten minutes after they got to the ambulance. Then they lit up their lights, turned on their sirens and were gone.

It was early evening when Rosa went back for the ATV and the cart. The light was still good, but the sun was in the southwestern sky, and it set some big blue clouds on fire. Those clouds glowed orange and red, showing off and proud of it. Nothing prettier than a sunset after a good rain.

She picked her way up the hill from the right of way. The downed trees blocked most of the woods road, but she would be able to snake around them with the ATV. She'd just have to go off road and zigzag through trees, dodging rocks and boulders.

She pulled the ATV back onto four wheels and then flipped the little cart onto its wheels.

Choke on. To Rosa's amazement, the ATV started right up. The woods road was clear for a hundred yards until you got to the slope with all those downed trees.

She was almost to the deer stand when she saw a bright orange box. The chainsaw, where she left it, lay hidden behind the log that had fallen on Collins. She turned the ATV's engine off and put the saw into the cart. The saw was heavy and it was clunky but now lifting it was cake, and nothing to be afraid of, because she, Rosa Bah, had used a chainsaw, cut a log in two places, and helped rescue her old white man boss.

That was when she noticed the deer stand. And climbed it one more time.

The air was clean and cool after the rain. It was just a little nicer up that tree. Rosa could see what a mess the burst had made of the woods, but she was also a lot closer to the setting sun. She could see fifteen or twenty downed trees, some of which had fallen on top of one another. Lots of work to clean this mess. Lots of time with a chainsaw. Not her thing, though. Chainsaws are too loud, too violent. Once was more than enough.

This time she was ready to relax. She took her smokes out of her top pocket. Somehow the pack had kept them dry. She took one out, lit it and inhaled deep. Satisfying. The pause that refreshes.

Plenty-plenty mess all afternoon. A niece had come to drive Mrs. Collins into town after the ambulance screamed off. They left Rosa alone with storm's wake. She cleaned up what she could. There were signs down and she brought them into the barn. The banners were wrapped around poles and one of the tractors, so she unraveled them and restrung any banners that weren't ripped to shreds. She walked through the strawberries and picked up trash barrels that had been knocked over. She put all the berries out in the store back into the refrigerator, hoping that the power would come back on, which it did after a few hours. Then she put the cash away and locked the store.

Mrs. Collins called her cell a few times. First, they were in the emergency room, in the trauma section. Then they were giving Mr. Collins blood and taking him to the operating room. Then Mr. Collins had had a heart attack from losing so much blood, but they thought he'd be okay. Then Mr. Collins was out of surgery and was going to the surgical ICU.

Rosa didn't know what to make of the updates. Mrs. Collins was treating her like family, and she wasn't family. Mr. Collins was a gruff old white guy. He was decent enough. She thought he was fair, but that man lived for work. Rosa could work as hard as anyone, but she wasn't about work. None of it really made sense.

She finished the smoke and smashed the butt on the metal bar she was leaning on until she was sure all the fire was out. Then she let the cigarette butt fall, and watched it tumble, end over end into the forest floor below, her purple lipstick coating one end.

All this farming, all this country life weighed on Rosa. It was a living, but it wasn't her. She'd stay a few weeks; long enough to find out if Collins was going to live or die and long enough to help Mrs. Collins until the season ended, but that was all.

It was time to move on with her life.

Second ending:

"You leave me here and I'm gonna die," Collins said. 'I'm bleeding to death inside my goddamn boot. My leg is broke. I can feel the bone poking through the skin and my foot feels like it's sitting in water. I bet that's blood not water and this trembling is what happens when a person goes into shock. There's no help that's coming up this road soon. We had a good burst and trees are down everywhere. If you don't cut me loose now that help will only get to reclaim the body, and that body would be mine."

"I'll call for help," Rosa said. Her cell phone was wet but it was still on. One bar.

"Call away," Collins said. "Then pick up that chainsaw and I'll talk you through cutting me loose."

I don't have to pay that man no heed, Rosa thought. *He can't get up and take after me. He old. Maybe he die and quit ordering me here and there. No more do this and that.*

She lifted the chainsaw anyway. Heavy old thing. Too heavy to use. Makes a bad noise. No woman in her right mind would touch that thing.

"Bring that saw here now," Collins said. The man was white and sweaty. Rosa could see how the pain crept up inside him, under his skin, in his eyes, in his brain, how it made him tense and needy.

She brought the saw and put it on the ground just out of Collins' reach. Then she backed away.

"You flip the start switch … to on," Collins said. He was pale as a ghost and had to pause for breath.

Rosa backed away. Collins reached for the saw and groaned again as the bad leg shifted inside his boot. Then he became quiet and stopped moving. More white. Then gray. He gasped. Once. Twice. Three times. Then he went blue.

Rosa met the rescue people on the hillside. They had a gurney, but it got stuck when they got to the part of the road where all the trees were down.

"Quick-quick," Rosa said when she saw them. "He this way. Bad."

The rescue people pulled a backboard off the gurney and tried to run through the woods. One was young and fat. He carried a big orange box. Two were women, one thin as a reed and one with a broad pear-shaped bottom but she ran good anyway. The thin woman carried a small green box. The last one was a square man with big shoulders and a big belly. He couldn't run much at all.

"Oh shit," the man with the shoulders and belly said. "Walter Collins."

They threw Collins on his back. One of them squatted next to him, locked her arms and pushed into his chest, rocking back and forth has she jammed his chest down. Another opened the orange box and took out a clear round plastic contraption that he used to cover Collins's face. She squeezed the contraption in time to the lady who was pushing on Collins' chest, one squeeze for ten or fifteen pushes.

"Shock him," the thin woman who was in charge said. She got a pair of scissors from the orange box and cut through Collins's shirt and jacket, exposing his bare white skin. He had white hair on his chest. Lots of hair. Rosa was surprised. She would have thought he had no hair on his body, that his body was thin, pink and smooth, like a capsule with medicine in it. The thin woman opened the green box, took out some patches and wires, and put the patches on Collins's chest.

"Clear," she said.

The other backed away and Collins's body jumped. Then the rescue people pounced on him again.

"No pulse, no respiration," the pear-shaped woman said. 'Begin CPR." They started pounding on Collins's chest and squeezing the contraption on his face again.

It was the big-shouldered man who started up the chainsaw and cut Collins' body loose after they gave up trying to bring that dead man back to life. They cut Collin's body free. Then they put him on the backboard and carried him out of the woods, one of his arms dangling from the backboard as they carried the body back to the gurney.

Rosa stood for a moment and watched them go. She couldn't take her eyes off the dangling arm, which swayed and jiggled as if no one owned it, as if it were a puppet on a string that no one controlled.

Then she went to get the ATV. She pulled it back onto all four wheels. It started right up.

On the way back, she noticed the chainsaw, which the rescue people had left on a stump close to the deer stand. She put the saw in the cart and looked up at the deer stand again.

I'm not climbing that stupid deer stand again, Rosa thought. No need to now.

No more deer stands for me, she thought. No deer stands, no chainsaws, no farmer and no farm.

She was more than ready for a different life.

The Social Determinants of Health

Brigetta was strong and ready when her sister Marianna came to Brigetta's house to die. Eduardo died a year before Marianna came. If God had made Brigetta, Hector, and her children strong enough to survive the death of their brother and son, then they could also take care of Marianna, although watching her sister die was the last thing Brigetta thought she would ever have to do.

Brigetta lived in Johnston in a new white house with a yard, a swing-set, and an above-ground pool in the back, with trees that had been recently planted and were starting to grow. There were no other people of color in their housing development. All the houses looked the same except for the colors of the houses and the different cars, pickup trucks, and boats parked out front. Brigetta had a red riding mower in the garage just like everyone else. She had Hector, who went to work and came home every day and smiled almost all the time. And she had still had Joao and Ana to keep her strong. Brigetta had to be strong for her kids and she had to be strong for Hector. Joao and Ana had to get to school every day despite what was happening at home because they had to learn and grow and be strong and make a life for themselves. No one else can live your life for you. The kids had to learn to stand on their own two feet.

Hector, Joao, and Ana kept Brigetta strong even while Eduardo was dying. Once Brigetta had been in charge. Brigetta made the meals, did the shopping, paid the bills, made sure the kids got to school and to soccer practice on time. Now everyone was in charge together.

When Eduardo first got sick, Brigetta was able to keep doing it all. Get up, make breakfast and lunches, get everyone else up, get them to school, get to work, run the office, go to the bank, pick up after school, shop, make dinner, call everyone in, have dinner, put away from dinner, pay the bills, make sure the kids got to sleep on time. Hector was good to drop off one or two of the kids when they went to different schools, even though only Ana was his real daughter. Hector was reliable but that was all he could manage.

When Eduardo first got sick, Brigetta just added on the extra things. Doctor's visit here. Radiation there. Chemo. Just more to plan, organize, and do. Brigetta didn't really hear what the doctors told her, or maybe she just didn't believe it. Eduardo hurt his leg, that's all. Hurt legs get better. Eduardo was seventeen, her best student, famous for rock climbing and soccer and dancing, strong and bright and polite. Sometimes he persecuted his brother and his sister — more his sister than his brother — but Eduardo was going to have a strong and brilliant life. Everyone in his family, town, and community looked up to him. Eduardo showed them how good we are as people and how much we bring to this place, to this country.

Until it became impossible to add on and impossible not to hear. Until Eduardo stayed in the hospital. Then there was a remission for sixteen months and for a while everything went back to how it had always been. But then Eduardo had a relapse. The doctor — the small, tough, woman doctor who never really looked at Brigetta — said there was going to be a relapse. Brigetta didn't believe it. This cancer could not happen to Eduardo. It could not happen to her. It could not happen to them. Seventeen-year-old soccer stars don't get cancer. People get better from cancer.

Then they were in the hospital again, and at first Brigetta was there every moment she wasn't working. And then she was there every moment of every day. Time went fast and slow at once. Everything at home still happened anyway, even without her. The meals were made. The kids got to where they needed to go. The lawn got mowed. The shopping was done, and the bills were paid. Brigetta still ran her office — did the billing and the payroll and ordered supplies — from Eduardo's hospital room because there was no one else to do that, but the rest just happened. Hector drove and shopped and cooked and kept smiling as he worked even though there was no smiling in his eyes. Joao brought in Eduardo's schoolwork every day and cleaned the house. Ana, still young, kept her room clean and the computer off. They were together in the hospital most nights and on the weekends, in Eduardo's room, as his school friends and their community came and went and came again to visit by the hundreds, so that his room was filled with cards and balloons and flowers and plants and fruits, and when he could, Eduardo sat up in bed, gossiping and laughing and he did not let anything – the pain or the dread — show. Only love and dignity showed. Eduardo taught them. He had enough love and dignity for all of them, and he taught love and dignity to everyone who came near.

They don't understand us, our community or our families, Brigetta always told her kids. They are frightened by all the brothers and sisters. They don't know what to make of same ma, different pa; or same ma, same pa; or same pa, different ma. Of thirty-six brothers and sisters. Brigetta felt sorry for them, the others, with their one or two kids and their divorces and anger. She didn't ever explain. Her kids heard her talking to the neighbors, and her kids didn't explain either. Brothers and sisters. Aunts and uncles. All the cousins. Life was full enough without the neighbors. Still, the neighbors saw the cars coming to the house on the weekends. The neighbors' kids came and saw all the people in Eduardo's room. Brigetta knew that the others — the neighbors — worried, wondered, judged, and feared what they did not know or understand. But they came too, anyway.

Brigetta learned that nothing mattered besides Eduardo and being with him morning, noon, and night.

So when Marianna came to her house to die, Brigetta was ready. It was less than a year after Eduardo died. Life had resumed, less than it was before, but it was still life. Hector was tired and sometimes came home late. Ana and Joao stayed in their rooms, often with their doors closed. Brigetta moved through that time without thinking or remembering.

Then Ana and Joao came out of their rooms and began to do homework at the kitchen table and sometimes asked for help. Then there were kids at the door looking for Ana and Joao. Even so the house was quieter than before and in quiet moments you could still feel the sadness and loss rolling about in the corners of the rooms, like dust balls in a room no one had swept.

But the empty spaces soon filled with voices and the music and the chatter of those kids. Hector, Brigetta, Ana, and Joao planned a memorial concert, set up a scholarship fund, and raised money for the Cancer Fund. Brigetta was back in the office, and all the bills got paid. Sometimes they were a few weeks late mowing the lawn. You don't get time off to take a vacation and catch up after your son and brother dies at nineteen. You just keep living.

Marianna was a good sister, but she wasn't the closest. She had a man who wasn't that good, and three children. Two with the same man, one with a different man. She had sparkle. She finished high school by GED after the first baby and worked as a CNA in a nursing home in Warwick. It was not fair that she got breast cancer at thirty-two, because she was the one with the most pizzazz, the most dance. They could all dance, the whole family, but when Marianna danced you always watched out of the corner of your eye because she made you feel alive and jealous and even a little aroused. She danced with all of her. She danced with the full joy of living, even the good, dirty, sexual parts, and she made them all proud.

Marianna farmed out her children and kissed them goodbye. Two to sisters. One to the last man's sister. They would come by once a week to hug her. They had big eyes and no understanding about what was happening. Children don't understand. They just do, and then they make up stories for themselves about the places they have been put and why they have been put there.

Ana was good with those kids. She took them outside to the swing set and played with them while the adults sat in the living room, down the hall from where Marianna was dying. The sisters came and brought food. Brigetta walked in and out of Marianna's room, bringing in one person at a time.

Sometimes the men were there, but mostly the sisters came, the women. Their sister Carolina. Their sister Sarah. Their sister-in-law Ana, who was better than a sister most of the time. Their sister Ariana. Their sister Romana. Their aunt Maria, who was younger than Carolina and who grew up more a sister than an aunt. Maria would come Sundays, and sometimes she would bring the other aunts — Monica, Carla, Victoria and Yvette. The sisters brought the good things to eat that Brigetta passed out to the people sitting in the living room, but no one ate. The sisters stood together in the kitchen, while the aunts and uncles sat together in the living room and the kids ran in and out of the house and no one had the energy to look at one another, not really.

At night, and in the morning, Brigetta sat with Marianna. Marianna had pain. Marianna's lungs were filling. They put a catheter into one lung so Brigetta could drain the fluid out once a day. But the catheter was very tender and touching it made the pain worse, so Brigetta gave Marianna pills an hour before. The pain pills were every three to four hours, but sometimes, when Marianna cried out from breathing, Brigetta gave her the pills early. Sometimes Marianna slept between the pills. Sometimes Marianna dreamt, and sometimes she talked in those dreams and sometimes she didn't know where she was or who was there. Sometimes she talked Crioulo. Sometimes she cried out as if a man with a knife was cutting her. Sometimes she soiled the bed.

Sometimes they talked. There was a chair next to Marianna's bed. At night, when the house quieted, Brigetta sat next to the bed paying bills or doing the office billing on her laptop while Marianna slept. For a little while — a few hours after the last pill, and an hour before the next pill — Marianna was awake. Just a little while. Before the need for the next pill made her angry and tense.

"You are the strong one," Marianna said, one night.

"Not that strong," Brigetta said.

"I wish I lived in Johnston."

"You are living in Johnston now."

"I wanted a man like Hector."

"Hector is just a man. You had good men. Not good enough for you though. You have good kids."

Marianna began to cry.

Brigetta began to cry.

"They need a mother," Marianna said. "I love my kids."

"They will be strong," Brigetta said. "They will remember their mother, and they will be strong."

"There is no one…"

"We will be there," Brigetta said. "You are part of us. They are part of us. We love them and will always love them. The way we love you."

Then Brigetta's arms locked around Marianna's chest, and they were crying together. They held each other until it was time for the medicine. Until the medicine kicked in and Marianna's breathing slowed, and she slept.

Marianna died three days later.

The sisters and the aunts came. Hector was there and so were Joao and Ana. They were all standing about the house when the car came from Dove's.

A polite young woman in a dark suit rang the bell. It was the same woman who had been there for Eduardo. Brigetta opened the door and met the woman's eyes for a moment but looked away when she saw the woman recognized her as well. She didn't remember the woman's name. She had spoken to a man on the phone, a man who was also polite and somehow Brigetta hoped that it would be the man who came and not the woman.

"Mrs. DeCosta?" the woman said. "I'm Yvette Dove. I'm so sorry for your loss."

The woman was wearing white gloves which she left on when she was shaking Brigetta's hand. She reached over with her left hand and held Brigetta's hand between her hands. An embrace, not a handshake. The gloves were smooth and cool, like the cold polished stone of the counter in a government building.

"Thank you. Marianna is in the bedroom."

The woman came through the door and followed Brigetta down the hall, shaking the hands of everyone in the hall as she passed them and saying those words over and over: I'm sorry for your loss. I'm sorry for your loss. I'm sorry for your loss.

Marianna's eyes were closed, and she was quiet. She had lost so much weight, and her hair was just a few inches long — all that had been able to grow back after the last chemo. Brigetta could no longer see or feel the sadness and the struggle of the last few weeks, when Marianna had pushed back against death.

The woman touched Marianna's arm, and forehead.

"She's so young," the woman said.

Suddenly Brigetta realized that the woman and Marianna were about the same age, and probably knew one another growing up.

But the woman did not pause.

"Cancer?"

"Cancer. Yes cancer. Only eleven months," Brigetta said. "She was hospice."

"Hospice called. Who was her doctor?" the woman said. "For the death certificate."

Brigetta gave the name of the doctor.

"I'll get the gurney," the woman said.

Brigetta stayed in the bedroom. Marianna was young but so gaunt. There was a sweet smell in the room, like the smell of the wood of a tree that had just been cut and split, the smell of sap, of growing things.

The woman came back with a man in a dark suit and a gurney. They lowered the gurney so it was just a little lower than the bed and then rolled up the sheet on the nearside of the bed so it was touching Marianna's left side and stood next to Brigetta.

"One, two, three, pull," the woman said, no louder than a whisper.

Brigetta closed her eyes to be strong. Then everything disappeared.

There were people. Strong hands under Brigetta's arms. Voices giving orders. Strong arms lifting her back and legs. Voices calling out. Arms around her, holding her close.

And then Brigetta felt herself rising, as if she were lighter than air and untethered, rising through the air all alone. She floated above the telephone poles and the wires that ran from one to the next. She alone was in the sunlight. The air was sweet. There was nothing holding her back, and she floated higher, floating free through the air above the trees, looking back on the earth and all its beauty. Where was everyone she loved?

When Brigetta awoke, she was laying on the couch in the living room, and her sisters and her children were holding her. Hector was kneeling next to her, holding a moist compress on her forehead.

Everyone was there with her.

They were together now, and they were strong, strong as trees, strong as mountains, strong as the earth and perhaps even stronger than death itself.

The Blind Emperor

Nothing is the way it used to be.

Once upon a time, Federal Hill was for Italians. The Episcopalians and the Quakers lived on College Hill. The Jews lived in South Providence and Smith Hill. Mount Hope was Black. Fox Point was Portuguese and Cape Verdean, although to tell the truth, we thought the Cape Verdeans were Blacks who didn't get the part about Mount Hope. The French Canadians lived in Woonsocket, Central Falls and Pawtucket. The Polish lived in Central Falls. The Greeks lived in Cranston. The Irish lived everywhere else, and there were no Dominicans, Puerto Ricans, Colombians, Guatemalans, Mexicans, Salvadorians, Nigerians, Liberians, Ghanaians, Sierra Leoneans, Hmong, Cambodians, Nepalese or Malians – nothing like that. Life was simpler then. You knew who was who and what was what. A man was a man. A woman was a woman. A kid was a kid. One plus one still equaled two. No new math. No finessing. You knew who you were and what you were and what to expect. Even when it sucked. Which it did sometimes, for some people. And for some people way more than others. But most of us, we took what we were given, loved who we loved, hated who we hated, and just sucked it up when shit happened. Which it did. Often. In the days before you could write and say curse words in public, before women even knew what they had was called a vagina and before men knew that they were supposed to think and feel, to be anything other than brutes.

Abe Klein inherited the place. It was the family business, a business that came to Abe when his father, the reigning Blind Emperor, had a stroke at 83. Abe never imagined he'd be back in Providence or ever have anything to do with the Blind Emperor again, but here he was.

The Blind Emperor was the inspiration and invention of Abe's great-grandmother Sophie, a short, squat, swarthy Yiddish speaking woman from Russia–Poland, who came steerage to the US with two infants in 1902. Sophie followed her husband of five years from Poland to Danzig, to Ellis Island, to the Lower East Side, and then to Providence, where she found that husband was living on Orms Street with a new wife and two new babies on the third floor of a triple-decker in a two-room cold-water flat.

So Abe's great-grandmother Sophie found her own cold-water flat. She took in piece-work jewelry and washing to survive, working for women who themselves had to work twelve or fourteen hours a day in retail or making jewelry or in one of Rhode Island's hundreds of mills, mills that made worsted wool, locomotives, screws, underwear or wire.

Before long, the husband of some of the women Sophie washed for bought houses. Some of those houses had venetian blinds. Those blinds needed to be cleaned once or twice a year. Soon those women's husbands started to take down the venetian blinds in the spring and fall, carry them over to Sophie's house, and Sophie cleaned them. And thus, a business was born.

The Blind Emperor. Sophie might have been short and squat. She might have worn dark European clothing in all the pictures Abe had of her. She might have had glasses with bottle thick lenses, but she also had a certain grandiose style — she wanted all her family and friends to know how successful she was in America, and how important she and her family had become, despite the disgrace of her abandonment by her husband. So it wasn't the Blind Store. Or the Venetian Blind Shop. Or even Window Coverings International. No. It was The Blind Emperor. A name that made it clear Sophie was a woman to be reckoned with, and that Sophie was in control.

Abe never knew his great-grandmother, of course. She died at 56 of stomach cancer, worn down by a life of toil, stress and physical labor.

Sophie's son, Abe's grandfather Sol, worked in the Blind Emperor his whole life as well. Abe's father Manny went to Brown and almost escaped. He was a socialist, and for a brief period, a member of the Communist Party. His degree was in European History with a concentration in the revolutions of 1848. He went to law school in 1938. Then the Second World War broke out, Abe's father enlisted and was sent to the Pacific. When the war ended, Abe's grandfather couldn't find help in the shop and so Abe's father came home and worked in the store just to tide his father over. But one day led to the next and Abe's father stayed. He became the Blind Emperor himself, the man to come to, for blinds, on the East Side of Providence, in Barrington and East Greenwich and even as far away as Newport and Fall River and the South Shore. The emperor of all the blinds he could see.

Abe, on the other hand, was a different sort of human being. He was an intellectual, and esthete, a child of the sixties, and he wanted no part of the family business. He learned to read at four and read everything he could get his hands on. He went to Classical High School but almost flunked out. He frustrated his teachers because they could tell he knew the answers to their questions, and often knew more about the material they were teaching than they did, but he couldn't be bothered to hand in the assignments, take tests, talk in class, or write papers.

Then Abe spent five years in a VW minibus as an anti-war dead-head, traveling around the US, stoned out of his mind. Five lost years. No memory at all of what had happened, of where he'd been or what he'd done other than gauzy dreams and occasional flashbacks, all out of context.

And then suddenly, coherence. Abe awoke one day in the East Village as a clerk at the Strand bookstore, living on East 7th Street between Avenues C and D, shelving some books and taking others home to read. He read and he learned. One day he got to talking with a brilliant young woman in a tight black top about Walter Benjamin. She told him about the New School, which was just a few blocks away on 13th Street, and invited him to sit in on a course she was teaching. He learned that Hannah Arendt, Erich Fromm and Hans Jonas taught at the New School. Then he started taking their courses, and before he knew it, Abe had become an unreconstructed European intellectual of the Frankfurt School, with a PhD in Philosophy and an interest in Epistemology and Critical Theory, teaching at NYU and the New School. He smoked like a fiend, gesticulated with his hands when he spoke, marched with the Socialist Internationale whenever they marched, and spent his evenings in obscure bars like the Frog Pond and the Ukraine National Home and Restaurant, discussing the fine points of the Hegelian roots of Marxist thought and the anarcho-syndicalist theory of science with colleagues and students from all over the country and the world.

Abe lived with a succession of women in those years, one more distracted and depressed than the next. Somehow, beautiful women were attracted to him, although Abe himself was nothing to look at — hunched over, bearded and bald, with bottle thick glasses like his grandmother's, beady eyes and pasty skin, part intellectual, part stevedore and part Talmudist. Women were pulled in by Abe's complete absorption in the world of ideas. But Abe never noticed women and he paid no attention to the women he lived with. The more beautiful the woman, the more she couldn't resist the temptation to be seen, to be noticed and to be known by Abe. But for Abe, women were a distraction from his real work, and he paid them no mind, even when one moved in for a few months and tried her best to make Abe look at her and see into her soul.

Except for one. Lily. Lily the Mexican poet-in-exile. They met one May in Tompkins Square Park, playing speed chess on the first warm day of spring, when the pigeons were everywhere, circling over the park. Lily was dark-haired and dark-complected with brilliant eyes that were more black than brown. She was a fierce chess player. She beat Abe five games in a row, with each successive victory taking her less time so that Abe was on his knees, from the perspective of chess, inside an hour, as Lilly quickly learned how his mind worked and used that knowledge to demolish his game.

Abe was mesmerized so he pursued Lily — the first time in his life Abe had put any effort at all into a relationship with a woman. He brought her flowers. He called her. He waited on the front stoop of her building on East Second Street until she came home at 4 AM, as the dawn was breaking over the East River. He took her out, once, on the Staten Island Ferry, to an Italian place on the Staten Island waterfront, and once, on the back of a motorcycle to the Delaware Water Gap, to the river between New Jersey and Pennsylvania. He drove all the way to Mexico City when she went home to stay for two months in the winter, when she got tired of the cold.

Truth be told, Abe and Lily were more alike than different. They were both the great-grandchildren of immigrant Eastern European Jews. Both lived in a world distant from the world most people lived in, a world of ideas, abstractions, and unique vocabularies, and both believed the world we have is not the world they wanted to live in, that the world needed improvement, which they were somehow empowered to try to create.

But Abe, try as he might, failed to win Lily's heart. He spent so much time in his own head, and had so many distractions that, though he was given to grand gestures, he was never really present when he and Lily were together. What all those other women fell in love with when they fell in love with Abe was Abe's absence. What Lily wanted was his presence. Or perhaps a different kind of presence all together, a man who would make her knees shake whenever he walked into a room. And Abe was just not that kind of man.

One day, when he was out marching down Fifth Avenue protesting one invasion or another, Lily moved her things out of Abe's apartment, and he never saw her again. He wondered for a bit when she wasn't home when he got home. It took two days for him to figure out that she had gone.

The sixties became the seventies; the seventies became the eighties, and then the nineties and then Y2K. The New York Abe knew transformed itself from a place of the heart and the mind to a place of steel and money, where graffiti was replaced by skyscrapers, where there were flowers in all the flowerbeds and the parks were clean and safe instead of scruffy and real. US colonialism didn't disappear. It just faded away, replaced by a new kind of capitalism and a new kind of materialism. The global economy. Money and work, not ideas, justice, beauty, family, friends, and love. Technology driving the human experience, just like Marx said it would. No class consciousness. Not even any classes, not really. Just consumers. No life of the mind.

Then, out of this sad coherence, chaos again. Abe's father had a stroke. Someone needed to run the store until they could wind things down and sell the building. No one cleans venetian blinds anymore. Yes, they had moved into window fashions. Yes, they had every size and color of mini-blinds imaginable – and custom awnings, drapery, canopies, motorized window coverings, quilted curtains to keep in the heat, tinted applications that let in only certain wave-lengths of sunlight – you name it, and the Blind Emperor had it or could get it overnight. Abe's father had done a bang-up job, keeping the Blind Emperor up to speed in the market, becoming the Blind Emperor in fact.

Abe would run the place for a week, not a month. Until Abe and sister could get Abe's parents situated. But not one day more than that, until they could figure out how much function Abe's father had lost and how much might come back.

A week turned into a month. A month turned into a year. One year turned into ten.

To his surprise Abe found he liked the work. He liked the challenge of keeping track of ten different things at once. He liked running numbers in his head. Abe worked in the store in high school, and knew how to run the business, almost instinctively, as though venetian blinds were his genome. He knew how to check inventory and order stock. How to keep your eye on your employees, because if you turn your back for one second even the good ones will steal from you. How to do payroll and make bank deposits, make sure payroll taxes are paid and the income tax filings are done on time.

He loved his employees and loved hearing about their lives which were sometimes chaotic but more often were lives of hard work, family love and human decency. There were even some customers he liked, even though most were made-up young women from the suburbs who drove him crazy. Their materialism was part of the problem. But their thousands of questions and constant negotiation — for a better price, a better color, about the time of day of delivery and so forth made Abe despair for the human condition, the same old despair that he used to think about abstractly when he read the newspaper in the morning, only now was a despair that was present close-up and personal every single day. Reified. That was the word that Kant or Heidegger or even Habermas would have used. Abe's world was real now. In a way he never planned for or anticipated.

One day at noon, when Abe was in the store by himself, a young woman came into the store alone. She had tan skin, deep brown eyes that were more black than brown, and long pink-and-blue hair that had once been almost black. She was much younger than most of the women who came into the store. Than all of the women who came into the store. Probably ever.

She came right to the counter. Pierced lips, nose, cheek, and eyebrow. Tattoos everywhere. Maybe she was after a handout. Lots of drug addicted people on the street now. The imminent collapse of capitalism. Better she asks than steals, at least from him, Abe thought. She could be anyone or anything. But more likely trouble than not.

Abe sat off to the side, reading *The Monthly Review*. He let the young woman stand at the counter while he finished reading an essay. It's a good idea to let customers stand and look for a few minutes, so they can decide what they are interested in. Although this young lady didn't look anything like a customer to Abe.

"Hey," she said at last.

Abe raised his eyebrows and looked at her over his glasses. Hey? Hey? This wasn't a grownup. Abe had been to lots of places, but he couldn't recall ever being addressed as "Hey" in all his years of teaching and all those demonstrations. "Yo" perhaps, but never "Hey." On the other hand, he had been in the store for ten years, and was probably out of touch. But still.

"May I help you?" Abe said. He stood and walked to the counter.

"I'm with *Allidos*. We are a confederation of community organizations, providing support for new immigrants and victims of hate crimes and state-sponsored violence in Rhode Island and southern New England," the young woman said. Her tongue was pierced too. She had a hint of an accent, but not one Abe could place.

"Uh huh," Abe said.

"We are doing a community picnic as a fundraiser to raise money for our anti-racist, anti-fascist work. Do you have any food or supplies you can donate? Either for the fundraiser or to help us care for undocumented families," the young woman said.

The young woman looked wild and crazy, but she talked like a college kid. There was something vaguely familiar about her. That was strange. Abe hadn't been around college kids in ten years, and for the ten years before that it had been mostly graduate students. His graduate students tended to be scruffy and intense. The women were partial to light black tops and jeans, the men to leather jackets, and they all tried to look like they were working class. But not like this. And no piercings.

"You go to RISD?" Abe said.

"Brown," the young woman said.

"This is a window treatment store. We sell mini blinds. Curtains. Motorized window treatments. Stuff like that. Nothing of much use to undocumented people. Or that will be of any help in the anti-racist work, I'm afraid."

When Abe said the work "anti-racist" the young woman looked at him suspiciously, as though she had never heard an adult use that word before. Was he yanking her chain?

"Would you consider being a sponsor for the fundraiser? We have different levels – platinum, gold, silver and bronze," the young woman said.

"Platinum, gold and silver. Pretty capitalist ideology for anti-capitalist folks. Hierarchal structure, like the class system. Kind of a contradiction, don't you think?" Abe said.

The young woman looked at Abe like he had just walked out of a lunar lander. Human perhaps, but definitely from outer space. He was coming from a way different place than she expected. This was a wall covering store.

"Huh. Brown. Where are you from? Bet you come from money yourself," Abe said. He had a sudden sense of deja vu, as though this was a conversation he'd had once before, someplace in the distant past, or in a dream. The young woman had a certain mystery to her, a certain beauty that seemed oriental, as though a part of her was from a distant culture — and a part was intensely familiar. The pink-and-blue hair and the piercings were distractions from that beauty, but the beauty was clearly there, despite the young woman's attempt to cover it up.

"And why do you think having picnics and fundraisers are going to get rid of racism? Do you really believe you can go to a place like Brown, which was founded by slave traders, by god, and not be completely co-opted? Don't you know that's what Ivy League colleges are for? To take people with just a spark of intelligence, originality, and rebellion in them, and grind them down, burying them under volumes and volumes of academic claptrap and a zillion pages of distractionary rhetoric, to convince you that you are incapable of thinking for yourself," Abe said.

"Say what?" the young woman said. "I came here to ask for a donation, not to get a lecture. You don't know the first thing about me. I might as well not be in the room. Who do you think you are?"

Huh, Abe thought. There's a little fight in this young woman after all, despite how she looks.

And at the same time, he thought, this feels familiar. I've had this argument before.

"What's your name, anyway? Where are you from?" Abe said.

"I'm Rose. Rose Levy. I'm from Cuernavaca. That's in Mexico," the young woman said. "And I come from culture, not from money. Full ride, if you must know. My people are artists, potters and poets. And yes, I'm a Mexican Jew."

A door that had been closed suddenly opened.

She was Lily's granddaughter. Of all the little shops in America, of all the stores and restaurants and gas stations in the good old US of A, Lily's granddaughter had walked into the stupid little store that Abe ran, almost fifty years after Lily had left him. And then she had the same fight with Abe that Abe and Lily used to have. Fifty years before.

Abe was too much of a materialist to think that there must be a god to make something like that happen, but he thought it anyway, at least for a moment. Then he pushed that thought away. There is a great synchrony in human affairs. Structural isomorphism. We are made a certain way. What brings us together once sometimes brings us together again. We are one people and joined at the hip, however much our greed and jealousies pull us apart. That is all logical and explainable. But there is also a coherence to our lives that feels unexplainable, that is deep and mysterious and powerful all at the same time.

You could say Abe Klein took Rosie Levy under his wing, or you could say Rosie Levy brought Abe Klein back from the dead. Abe came to all Rosie's demonstrations. She wouldn't let him drive her places, but if they met at a demonstration, she would let him drive her home. And let him take her to Gregg's for coffee and dessert.

Abe sat down on the pavement with her at the demonstration at the Wyatt when a truck tried to drive through the line and he got Maced. Rosie stood next to him while he sat on the grass next to the road and she held Abe's head as the medics washed his eyes with water and milk, until he could see again, and she drove him home that night in his car.

They talked. Or she talked and he listened. He was tempted to teach her a little philosophy, a little Plato, a little Kant, a little Hegel and a lot of Marx, but for once he kept his mouth shut.

She was young and full of dreams. There was nothing more Abe Klein wanted than to listen and feel her hope and energy, so he could dream again himself.

She told Abe all about her grandmother. Lily had never married. Her daughter Violetta was the child of a married gondolier Lily met in Venice, who had died 10 years before. Her life had been rich in family and in relationships, and she had never let herself be confined. Not to one man. One relationship. Or even one place or gender.

Soon Abe Face-timed with Lily, once, twice and then for a few minutes whenever he spent an hour or two with Rose. Lily hadn't changed. She had crow's feet around her eyes perhaps, but aside from that, she hadn't aged a day. Her eyes were still dark brown and almost black, and they seemed even more lustrous than ever, the door to a soul that was as deep as the sea and as glittering as the Milky Way.

Yes, she would come to Providence, she said, and Abe thought he could hear some excitement, and even a little yearning in her voice when she said that. But that was how she talked to everyone, to every man and woman she'd ever known. He'd be thrilled if she came, he said, and a part of him hoped she'd say, come to visit here. Come to Cuerna-vaca. But she didn't say that, and Abe was content to just see her and to hear her voice once again.

Abe was waiting for her first visit when Covid hit. He is still wait-ing patiently until people can travel again. He listens, sees the world as it is, and is still the Blind Emperor, but Abe is also now seeing and listening to the world as it is, not the way it was or the way he thinks it should be.

Glossary (for *From All Men*)

Aliyah – Literally, going up. Generally used to describe the honor of going to recite blessings before the reading of a portion of the Torah.

Amidah – Silent Prayer, the central prayer of Jewish liturgy, which usually consists of 18 blessings but the actual number said varies with time of day and day of the week. It is repeated at least three times a day during the week and four times on Saturday, and recited silently, standing up and facing east. When a minyan is present, it is usually repeated, chanted out loud by the person leading the service.

Bereshit – the Hebrew name of the book of Genesis.

Borachu – literally, blessing. A blessing repeated out loud early in each service, which functions as a call to prayer.
Daven – (verb) to pray.
Gabbai – the person who calls people to have the honor of saying blessings before the reading of the Torah.

Haysedonda – yiddishized contraction for "Hey, sit down there" a joking description of the shamesh.

JCC – Jewish Community Center, usually a building which often has a gym and a swimming pool and meeting rooms for Jewish community organizations, common in the larger Jewish Communities of the US.

Kaddish – a prayer about the holiness of G-d, repeated a number of times in each service, and said standing by those in mourning and by people on the anniversary of the deaths of loved ones. The Mourner's Kaddish can only be said when a minyan (ten men, or ten people, depending on the congregation) is present.

Kaddish D'Rabbanan – a version of the Kaddish that recognizes the importance of scholars, recited in Orthodox communities after a lecture on certain parts of Talmud, and in other communities as part of the morning service.

Kiddusha – a section of the Amidah (Silent Prayer) which is recited only when a minyan is present.

Kippa (s), *Kippas* (pl) – skull cap, yarmulka.

HIAS – Hebrew Immigrant Aid Society, an organization that looked after new Jewish immigrants a hundred years ago and again after the Second World War and the Holocaust, and then again when large numbers of Russian immigrants came to the US, in the 1980s and 1990s, and which advocates effectively for immigrants from many places today.

Maariv – the evening service, often combined with Mincha, the afternoon service

Mincha – the afternoon service.

Minyan – traditionally, the ten men required for a service that includes saying a number of important prayers out loud or at all and for reading the Torah. US conservative and reform congregations now count all people over thirteen or who have been bar or bat mitzvahed as constituting a minyan.

Mishaberah – (literally, blessing) used here to mean the blessing for the sick, which is said as part of the Torah service.

Pikuach nefesh – A principle of Jewish law derived from Torah and developed in the Talmud, that says other Jewish laws can be violated if doing so is necessary to save a life.

Shema – A one line prayer that serves as the central coda of Judaism. "Hear O Israel the Lord our G-d, the Lord is One" is a rough translation. It is repeated at least twice a day, is said by children as a bedtime prayer, and observant Jews try to have it on their lips at the moment of their deaths.

Shemoneh esrei – the Amidah, or Silent Prayer.

Shul – Yiddish colloquialism for synagogue.

Sephardic trope – the sung pronunciation of the Torah read in Hebrew used by Jews descended from those who lived in Spain and Portugal, communities that moved to Holland, Greece, Turkey, Italy and North Africa after the Spanish Inquisition. That pronunciation used by Jews in Eastern Europe is called Ashkenazi trope.

Shabbat Shalom – tradition shabbos greeting, literally, greetings/peace on this Sabbath.

Shabbos – The Sabbath, the central organizing feature of Jewish life.

Shamesh – traditionally, the warden or caretaker of the synagogue. Now used to describe the person who organizes a religious service. Originally and also the candle on a Hanukah menorah that is used to light all the other candles, which is the origin of the use of the word in synagogue life.

Shaharit – the morning service

Shtetl – Small Yiddish speaking community in Eastern Europe. The villages where Jews lived, next to but otherwise? separate from their non-Jewish neighbors.

Siddur – prayer book, singular, Siddurim (plural)

Talmud – 63 complicated books of what was originally oral law that was transcribed to text, commentaries on that law and stories about the law and the rabbis who complied it over many centuries, all developed from the law set out in the Torah.

Tallasim – (plural) *Tallis*, singular, Askenazi; *Tallit*, singular, Sephardic – prayer shawl, worn on shabbos.

Torah – The five books of Moses, written by a trained scribe's hand on a sheepskin scroll, which is read out loud on Monday, Thursday and Saturday (Shabbos). There is considerable ceremony attached to the reading of the Torah, and a significant body of Jewish law laying out the way it is to be read. Once upon a time, the law was read in the marketplace: Monday and Thursday were market days.

Yahrzeit – the anniversary of the death of a close loved one (parent child or spouse), when Kaddish is recited in the presence of a minyan.

About the Author

Michael Fine is a writer, community organizer, family physician, public health official, and author of *Health Care Revolt: How to Organize, Build a Health Care System, and Resuscitate Democracy –All at the Same Time, Abundance,* a romantic thriller set in Rhode Island and in Liberia in the aftermath of the Liberian Civil Wars of 1989-2003. *The Bull and Other Stories* was his first collection of short stories.

All the stories in *The Bull and Other Stories* and *Rhode Island Stories* are available as a podcast called **Alternative Fictions: New Stories from Michael Fine.** Find the podcast at https://linktr.ee/drmichaelfine.

All of Michael Fine's stories and books are available at: www.MichaelFineMD.com

Also by Michael Fine

ABUNDANCE

ISBN: 978162963-644-3

$17.95 • 5x8 •352 pages

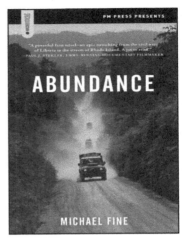

Julia is an American medical doctor fleeing her own privileged background to find a new life delivering health care to African villages, where her skills can make a difference. Carl is also an American, whose very different experiences as a black man in the United States have driven him into exile in West Africa, where he is an international NGO expat. The two come to- gether as colleagues (and then more) as Liberia is gripped in a brutal civil war. Child soldiers kidnap Julia on a remote jungle road, and Carl is evacuated against his will by U.S. Marines. Back in the United States he finds Julia's mentor, Levin, a Rhode Island MD whose Sixties idealism has been hijacked by history. Then they meet the thief. Then they meet the smuggler. And the dangerous work of finding and rescuing Julia begins.

An unforgettable thriller grounded in real events.

"Michael Fine's novel, *Abundance*, is a riveting, suspenseful tale of love, violence, adventure, idealism, sometimes-comic cynicism, class conflict and crime . . . a story that displays both the deep disconnect between the First and Third Worlds and our commonalities."
> —Robert Whitcomb, former finance editor of the *International Herald Tribune* and former editorial page editor of the *Providence Journal*

"Michael Fine takes us into the heart of a country at war with itself. But our journey, in battered Land Rovers, along potholed red dirt roads, is pro- pelled by love, not hate. That love offers hope for Liberia, our often forgot- ten sister country, and anyone who confronts despair. Read *Abundance*. Reignite your own search for a life worth living."
> —Martha Bebinger, WBUR

"A powerful first novel—an epic stretching from the civil wars of Liberia to the streets of Rhode Island. A joy to read!"
> —Paul J. Stekler, Emmy-winning documentary filmmaker

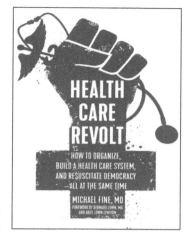

Also by Michael Fine

THE NATURE OF HEALTH

How America lost, and can regain,
a Basic Human Value
Foreword by Robert S. Lawrence M.D.

ISBN: 978036744-619-2

6x9 •264 pages

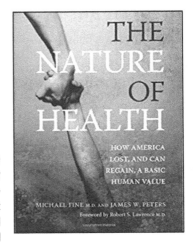

This pioneering work addresses a key issue
that confronts all industrialized nations: How
do we organize healthcare services in accord-
ance with fundamental human rights, whilst
competing with scientific and technological
advances, powerful commercial interests and
widespread public ignorance?

The Nature of Health presents a coherent, affordable and logical way to build a
healthcare system. It argues against a health system fixated on the pursuit of
longevity and suggests an alternative where the ability of an individual to function in worthwhile relationships is a better, more human goal.

By reviewing the etymology, sociology and anthropology of health, this contro-
versial guide examines the meaning of health, and proves how a community-
centered healthcare system improves local economy, creates social capital and
is affordable, rational, personal, and just.

"This is badly needed nourishment for a medical system glutted on technology, individ-
ualism, profit and the pursuit of longevity. Read and be fed."

—Christopher Koller, Health Insurance Commissioner, The State of Rhode Island,
USA.

"Unique. Surprising. A real eye-opener. Just about everyone who doesn't have a vested
financial interest in maintaining the status quo will agree that U.S. healthcare is badly
broken. [This book] is making it possible for us to refocus from how to provide
healthcare to how to achieve health. Their description of health as successful function-
ing in community, rather than as a measure of longevity is a definition that can make a
reader feel healthier as they take gradually appreciate the power of the concept. On
this foundation, it is not as hard as one might think to outline a healthcare system that
is equitable, affordable and achievable."

—Alexander Blount EdD, Professor of Family Medicine, University of Massachu-
setts Medical Center.

Also by Michael Fine

THE BULL AND OTHER STORIES
HC ISBN: 9781952521355
PB ISBN: 9781952521348

6x9 •146 pages

A bull gets loose in Tennessee. A black sergeant stops the murder of a Trump supporter in North Carolina. The third husband of a nurse in Pawtucket wins the lottery. A schizophrenic woman who lives on Kennedy Plaza discovers that Social Security thinks she is dead. The 19-year-old Latina caretaker of a rich old man loses her mother to COVID-19. A horse that represents the hopes and dreams of a family in India falls asleep, and then awakens.

Ten stories. People whose lives are transformed. People who struggle and survive, who see their world through lost hopes, inappropriate loves, and irrational dreams. Ten stories, each one a new way to listen, see, feel and dream.

"Michael Fine… is a master. From first sentence to last, this collection is a rare delight."
   —G. Wayne Miller, Staff writer at *The Providence Journal*

"Michael Fine's short stories rivet our readers… We can imagine them… pondering the obvious and the not s obvious life dramas that Michael writes that capture you from the beginning, to the very end."
   —Nancy Thomas, Co-founder and Editor, www.rinewstoday.com.

"Michael Fine's world is not fair but it is full. His characters are not beautiful but they have dignity… To read about them is to read about us."
   —Christopher F. Koller, President of the Millbank Memorial Fund

"Dr. Fine is a major writer."
   —Robert Whitcomb, President, The Boston Guardian, columnist for GoLocal24.com, and former financial editor of the *International Herald Tribune*.